Relationship.

It was a heavy word, and one that would have sent him literally running for the safety and anonymity of his beloved mountains.

Not this time.

This time, he wanted to stay.

It was Olivia who should be running, as far as she could go. He was no good for her. He didn't even know what a long-term relationship ought to look like. And as wonderful as he felt whenever he interacted with the triplets, he could hardly be the father figure they needed in their lives.

What did he know about being a father? Trying to pursue a long-term relationship was simply setting himself up for failure, and with that, Olivia and the triplets would also crash and burn.

What had he been thinking, spending all this time with Olivia? Giving her the wrong impression?

He hadn't been thinking at all. He'd been acting on his emotions.

He should end this relationship now—before it got too serious. It didn't matter that it was already serious to him. He wasn't who counted here.

* * *

Award-winning author **Deb Kastner** lives and writes in beautiful Colorado. Since her daughters have grown into adulthood and her nest is almost empty, she is excited to be able to discover new adventures, challenges and blessings, the biggest of which is her sweet grandchildren. She enjoys reading, watching movies, listening to music, singing in the church choir, and attending concerts and musicals.

Books by Deb Kastner

Love Inspired

Lone Star Cowboy League

A Daddy for Her Triplets

Cowboy Country

Yuletide Baby
The Cowboy's Forever Family
The Cowboy's Surprise Baby

Email Order Brides

Phoebe's Groom
The Doctor's Secret Son
The Nanny's Twin Blessings
Meeting Mr. Right

Serendipity Sweethearts

The Soldier's Sweetheart
Her Valentine Sheriff
Redeeming the Rancher

Yuletide Cowboys
"The Cowboy's Yuletide Reunion"

Visit the Author Profile page at Harlequin.com for more titles.

A Daddy
for Her Triplets

Deb Kastner

Special thanks and acknowledgment to Deb Kastner for her
contribution to the Lone Star Cowboy League miniseries.

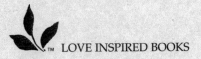

LOVE INSPIRED BOOKS

Recycling programs
for this product may
not exist in your area.

ISBN-13: 978-0-373-71933-4

A Daddy for Her Triplets

www.Harlequin.com

Printed in U.S.A.

There is no fear in love;
But perfect love casts out fear,
Because fear involves torment.
But he who fears has not been made perfect in love.
We love Him because He first loved us.
—*1 John* 4:18–19

To my Lord Jesus Christ. May every word I write always serve to glorify, adore and bring honor to my Savior. There would be no books without His Spirit working in and through my life.

Chapter One

"Olivia Barlow, as I live and breathe. Finally! There you are. I've been looking all over for you. I was beginning to think you weren't going to show up tonight at all. Then what would I have done?" Elderly Miss Betty Leland had clearly been watching for Olivia, because the sprightly old woman made a beeline for her the moment she herded her triplet six-year-old boys into the league's brightly decorated red-and-pink-crepe-papered banquet hall.

A cold finger of premonition skittered up Olivia's spine. Miss Betty was clearly up to something. Olivia could see it in the pale blue sparkle of the aged woman's eyes. Nothing good could possibly come out of that kind of mischief, however friendly and well-intentioned.

Olivia forced a laugh she didn't feel and returned the elderly woman's smile. It wasn't Miss Betty's fault Olivia wasn't in the mood for a party, especially Little Horn's Lone Star Cowboy League's Valentine Roundup.

Valentine's Day *anything* was more than widowed

Olivia wanted to deal with. She felt out of place here among seeking singles, newly engaged couples and newlyweds. It seemed as if everyone was in love except her—not that she wanted to be. She had her plate full to overflowing already.

The local band was warming up its fiddles, playing a lively Texas two-step for eager dancers. Various couples and hopeful single men and women were flooding into the Grange hall. There were also quite a few teenagers. The boys were roughhousing and trying to look cool for the groups of giggling girls watching them, but Olivia knew they hoped to pair up before the night was over.

She spotted Carson Thorn and Ruby Donovan, a newly engaged couple who were laughing together as they helped serve the punch. Engaged couple Finn Brannigan and Amelia Klondike were already testing out the dance floor. In a far corner away from the noisy speakers, Grady Stillwater stood with his grandma Mamie and his fiancée, Chloe Miner. Chloe was bouncing Grady's seven-month-old nephew, Cody, on her shoulder in time to the music.

Tyler Grainger, the local pediatrician, had recently married pretty Eva Brooks, and Olivia had heard they'd already started the process to adopt a baby.

Yep. Pretty much everyone but her—not that she minded. Much. Of course she didn't begrudge anyone their romantic happily-ever-after. She just didn't want to have to watch it. Not right now when her heart was still so tender after the loss of her own husband, Luke.

At least the planning committee had nixed the usual romantic mixing and matchmaking this year, what with all the problems the locals were having with recent thefts in the area. People were looking over their shoulders at every turn, afraid that what had happened to other ranches would happen to them.

It didn't make for a festive atmosphere, but the Lone Star Cowboy League had decided to go through with the dance nonetheless, perhaps to take folks' minds off their worries for a bit.

"If I'm being honest, I almost didn't come tonight," Olivia admitted, bending her head to speak into Miss Betty's ear. The woman was mostly deaf even without the loud din of music around her, although she'd never admit as much if you asked her. She just pretended she knew what a person was saying and then continued speaking to state her own fill of words.

Olivia brushed her dark brown curls behind her ear and gestured to her identical, towheaded sons, Noah, Levi and Caleb. "I probably would have passed on it, except the boys wouldn't let me off the hook. Apparently at school today they put a lot of effort into making Valentine's Day cards. They insisted they had to come to the dance in order to post them up on the Sweetheart Wall where their friends can see them. I just couldn't find it in my heart to say no to them."

The wall in question was already papered with hearts of all shapes, colors and sizes. In addition to hanging the schoolchildren's artwork, it was a town tradition for the adults in the crowd to publicly post their romantic notions and even the occasional marriage proposal. Over the years more than one engagement had come out of it.

Olivia was not in a place in her life where she was searching for romance, and she doubted she ever would be, between single-handedly raising her triplets and struggling to keep her small quarter horse farm afloat. Three boys and Barlow Acres was more than enough to fill her days. She fell into a dead sleep most nights, although occasionally rest would elude her and a spot of loneliness would creep in.

"I think it's some kind of competition between them and their classmates as to who made the most elaborate valentine," she continued. "Or at least a competition between the three of them. You know boys. The triplets like to make a contest out of everything."

Honestly, she found the whole thing to be more than a little ridiculous. What six-year-old boy wanted anything to do with a holiday steeped in romance and kissing? Her sons didn't even *like* girls yet, and wouldn't for a good long while. Several years at least.

She hoped.

"Well, good for them," Miss Betty replied, nodding so vigorously that her short gray curls bobbed in response. "I'm glad they pushed you off your farm and into the community for the dance. It's good for you to get out from time to time and mingle a little bit. It will do you a wealth of good. Mark my words."

She started to deny Miss Betty's statement but then realized that what the older woman was saying was spot-on. Olivia hadn't meant for that to happen, nor had she even been aware of her actions—or lack thereof. But she had to admit she'd been somewhat of a recluse lately. She hadn't been in the mood to participate in town activities nearly as much as she had before, but since her husband passed two years earlier, social activities just didn't seem the same.

Frankly, despite Miss Betty's kind words, Olivia wasn't sure it would do her any good to be at the party tonight. As stressed as she was about the farm, she was bound to be a downer in even the most mundane of conversations. It wouldn't lift her spirits, and in her current mood she wouldn't be much good to her friends.

There was a time in her past when she used to be social and upbeat, but at the moment it was all she could do not to break down in tears. The mortgage was due on the house, several of her mares were due to foal in the spring and she had no idea how she was going to come up with enough money to keep her dwindling herd in hay and oats until the horse market opened in early summer.

"Which reminds me," Miss Betty continued, either not recognizing Olivia's hesitation or refusing to acknowledge it. She reached into the oversize, glossy red purse dangling from the crook of her elbow and withdrew a small stack of folded pink and red heart-shaped notes. "Pink for the ladies, red for the gentlemen," she explained as she shuffled through them. As if that would mean something to Olivia—which it didn't. "Oh, here we go. Olivia Barlow."

Olivia automatically accepted the missive Miss Betty thrust at her. "Thank you. I—"

She stared down at the garish, fluorescent-pink, heart-shaped paper and her sentence abruptly stalled. Her name had been carefully stenciled onto the heart, but that wasn't what caught her eye. It was the name written beneath her own that kicked her adrenaline into overdrive.

Olivia Barlow

Clint Daniels

The floor fell out from underneath her and she gasped for breath against the sudden shock. Suddenly it was as if she were in junior high again, being paired up with a boy for square dancing by the physical education teacher. Philip Whitmore had been the boy's name, as she recalled, and he hadn't been able to dance his way out of a paper bag. Her toes had hurt for weeks afterward. Not her favorite memory.

But this was worse. Much worse. Even though she hadn't yet determined exactly what the *this* part of the plan was that Miss Betty had concocted, if it involved Clint Daniels, it couldn't be good.

"I don't understand," she muttered, trying without success to hand the note back to its owner.

"All in good fun, sweetie," Miss Betty assured her. "All in good fun. Just trust me on this. Your Miss Betty is looking out for your best interests. Find Clint. Talk to him. You may surprise yourself." She winked. "And him."

Oh, she would surprise him, all right, if she barreled up to him and tried to start a conversation right out of the blue, especially given the subject. Valentine cards. Matchmaking. Little old ladies with too much time on their hands.

Talk to Clint, huh? And say what, exactly? It wasn't as if they had anything in common. She wouldn't be able to come up with much more than saying hello to the man, and even that would be awkward in the extreme.

Clint was a surly, intimidating loner, a rough-edged man who preferred mountain living to spending time in town. He wasn't a people person. He didn't care for community events. In fact, she would be surprised if he even—

She hadn't even finished the thought when she glanced at the door and caught a glimpse of golden-haired Clint walking into the banquet hall, his foster mother, Libby Everhart, on his arm.

It figured. It just figured.

The one time Clint Daniels decided to show up for a town function and it had to be this one.

What a night Olivia was having. And the dance had barely started. If it was just her, she'd grab her coat and be out the door and into the cool air in a second. But with her boys here...

She was well and truly stuck.

She watched as Clint smiled casually and bent his head toward Libby to better hear what she was saying over the combined din of music and conversation. While Olivia didn't have any inclination to follow Miss Betty's suggestion, she had to admit he was handsome—in a rough kind of way. He wore his thick hair long enough to brush his collar and his hazel eyes were an intriguing blend of green and gold. He hadn't shaved in a couple days, and scruff shadowed the sharp planes of his cheeks and chin. Tall with broad shoulders, he looked every inch the mountain man he was.

She imagined his rugged good looks appealed to some women, but she didn't count herself among them. Her late husband, Luke, had been clean-cut, with a gentle gaze and winsome smile. Those were the kinds of features that attracted Olivia.

Clint's expression wasn't unkind, but it certainly couldn't be described as gentle. His smile was extremely confident, possibly even tipping the scale into arrogant territory.

She couldn't help the grin that crept up the corners of her lips as she watched him with his foster mother. Clint wouldn't be smiling in a moment. Miss Betty was headed straight toward him with his valentine missive in her hand.

A woman on a mission. A *matchmaking* mission.

Olivia chuckled. At the very least it would be an amusing exchange, and her gaze lingered. Could she help it if she wanted to watch the show?

A show that directly involved *her*.

Heat rushed to her face and she quickly turned away, her stomach churning. What was she thinking? As humorous as Clint's reaction would be, it was hardly something she'd want to see. How embarrassing. He probably wouldn't be rude to an old lady, but she suspected he'd toss the paper heart with her name on it into the trash can the moment Miss Betty turned her back. What a humiliating notion.

Leaving the dance altogether was sounding better and better by the moment. Now would be good.

Olivia searched for her sons and found them still lingering by the Sweetheart Wall, but they were no longer interested in the notes pinned there. Instead, they were rolling around on the floor and wrestling with each other, their hard work on their valentines long forgotten.

"Where are the cards you made?" she prompted, affectionately ruffling Noah's hair as he got to his feet, and separating Levi and Caleb.

Noah proudly pointed to the wall where a jaggedly cut heart was written on in pencil with large, uneven print. Several of the letters held telltale smudges indicating they had been erased and rewritten. But it was the words themselves that caused Olivia's heart to drop into her stomach and her throat to clog with emotion.

For: My New Daddy
Love, Noah

She didn't have to ask where Levi and Caleb's valentines were located. She found them easily. Close to the bottom of the board where little ones' hands could reach, they were the only two on the wall with the same request as Noah's.

For a father.

The one thing she could not give them. She would do anything for her boys. Anything. But some things were beyond her control.

Her heart ached for her boys, partly because they'd known grief at such a young age, having lost their father to an accident, and also because she was painfully aware that she could not fulfill their wishes. She had no clue how she was supposed to explain to them that she wasn't looking to get remarried. They wouldn't equate their idea of getting a new daddy with the fact that, in the process, she'd have to find a new husband. They were only six years old. How could they possibly understand?

She didn't want them to know anything about the strain she was under. She wanted them to grow up innocent and happy. With the death of their father, they'd had to mature far too much already. She worried about their not having a good male role model in their lives, but there was little she could do to change that, at least not at present and possibly never. Male friends and neighbors would have to do.

"What's that, Mama?" Levi asked, pointing to the crumpled heart in her fist. She'd forgotten she was still holding it. "Did you get a valentine? Who's it from?"

"I—no—" she stammered, but Caleb had already loosened her grip enough to pry the paper away.

"It says Mama and Mr. Clint!" Caleb exclaimed. He was the best reader of the three and had no problem sounding out the words. This one time she wished that he wasn't quite so good at it.

The triplets simultaneously broke into excited chatter about Mama's valentine.

"Boys, please." She felt as if she was watching a spark skittering down a long fuse toward a barn full of explosives. "This isn't…" She frowned and lowered her brows. "Wait. How do you guys know Clint—er—*Mr.* Clint?"

"He came to our class," Levi explained.

"Yeah," Caleb added. "He talked about camping and rock climbing and horseback riding and search and rescue. He is so cool, Mama. He works in the Deep Gulch Mountains. I want to work in the mountains."

"And he even brought his dog, Pav," Noah exclaimed, talking over his brothers. "Pav is a golden 'triever. He likes to catch balls in his mouth."

"Pav?" Olivia was barely keeping up with the babbling triplets, but it didn't take a genius to add the boys' thoughts together and come up with a frightening sum.

One man plus one woman plus three young boys and a dog named Pav.

Oh, no.

"Boys," she said, hoping the tone of her voice alone would corral their high spirits. But it was too late. With a whoop and a holler they took off, sprinting across the room as fast as their legs could carry them.

Straight toward Clint without a single detour.

From bad to worse to a total disaster in a matter of seconds.

Olivia groaned and absently combed her fingers through her hair, then realized what she was doing and immediately dropped her hands to her side. She was not going to worry about how her hair looked, or if her makeup had smeared, because it didn't matter how Clint saw her. His perceptions wouldn't make a bit of difference to her.

That was her story and she was going to stick to it.

Clint kept his hand on his foster mother's elbow, not so much because she needed an escort as that he did. This whole Valentine Roundup thing made him antsy and uncomfortable, even if the league had promised there'd be no matchmaking this year. At a mixer like this with most if not all the members of the Lone Star Cowboy League and their families present, there were bound to be single women on the prowl for a husband, and Clint wasn't interested. He was a confirmed bachelor with a capital *B*.

He was not in the market for a wife. Unfortunately, women weren't so quick to pick up on that.

He'd had a few relationships over the years, but it never worked out long term—and he readily admitted he was the reason. He'd start dating an attractive woman only to have her go and get all serious on him, usually sooner rather than later. She'd start pushing him to "define the relationship." Or worse yet, she'd go and use the *L* word. Even the thought made him shiver.

He didn't like feeling boxed in, and there was nothing like a woman trying to hog-tie him to make him claustrophobic. Freedom to come and go as he pleased was paramount to him. Women just didn't get that. Or want it.

Which suited him just fine. He liked his life the way it was. His golden retriever, Pav, was all the company he needed. Marriage and family? He had nothing to offer.

As they passed through the room, Clint took a moment to shake hands with Grady Stillwater, a wounded ex-army special ops buddy who, up until recently, had also been a certified bachelor—at least until he'd fallen head over heels for his physical therapist, Chloe Miner. Now, suddenly, he was all but crowing about the virtues of matrimony.

"How's Ben?" Grady's twin brother, Ben, had been in a horse riding accident that had left him in a coma for several months. Thankfully, he'd recently awakened, but he'd had a mini stroke and was fighting to regain full use of all his faculties.

"Grumpy," Grady replied with a shrug. "Which Chloe tells me is a good sign. He's getting better every day."

Clint clapped a hand on Grady's shoulder. "Glad to hear it, man."

Clint returned his attention to Libby, who was deep in conversation with the elderly Miss Betty Leland. He didn't realize Miss Betty was speaking to him until Libby swatted him on his biceps with her palm.

"Clint, pay attention," she admonished. Libby Everhart was the one and only woman who ever got to tell him what to do. He loved her like a mother and she'd earned his respect. "Miss Betty just asked you a question."

"Yes, ma'am. I apologize, Miss Betty. My mind was miles away. You were saying?"

"Just wondering where your thoughts were, sweetheart. Oh, and I wanted to give you this."

Clint automatically took the paper heart Miss Betty offered him, although he couldn't fathom why she would want to give him a valentine. Oh, well. He couldn't help it if his natural charm affected ladies of all ages. He gave her his best grin.

"Got your perfect match on it," she explained.

"My *what*?" The smile dropped from his face.

"Be a good sport." Libby's voice held a note of warning he couldn't ignore.

"I—er—okay." There went any possibility of getting through this night unscathed. He watched his freedom fly right out the window along with any peace he'd hoped to maintain.

He glanced at the paper and immediately wished he hadn't. He took a breath and choked on it.

Olivia Barlow

Clint Daniels

What was *that* about? Miss Betty couldn't possibly think he ought to spend time with Olivia Barlow. The very thought was preposterous. Olivia being a match for Clint was about as far out for him as suggesting the moon was made of green cheese. The woman was a widow with three young sons. Surely Miss Betty didn't think *he'd*—

"Just talk to her," Miss Betty said with a crisp, knowing nod and a mischievous sparkle in her pale blue eyes. "That's all I'm asking."

Oh, so that's *all* it was.

On what planet? Clint wanted to huff in protest, but with Libby there, he didn't dare.

"Ask her to dance," Libby said in a tone that was much too severe to be a mere suggestion. How was he supposed to ignore the *mother* voice? Clint winced inwardly.

What could Libby be thinking, agreeing with Miss Betty in this? And why were they ganging up on him?

His asking Olivia anything was *so* not going to happen, no matter what the older ladies thought was best for him. He had no inclination whatsoever to spend time with the triplets' mama, even if she was a pretty woman with dark brown curls and sea-blue eyes. No one outside of Miss Betty—and Libby, apparently—would fault him for sitting this one out.

He scanned the room. Maybe Olivia wouldn't even be here. A man could hope.

But no. There she was, over by the Sweetheart Wall, her palms pressed to her flaming cheeks.

And she was staring right at him.

Of course she was. Miss Betty had probably delivered an identical missive to her.

Their gazes met and locked. His heart thudded in an irregular tempo, but he refused to be the first to look away. He raised an eyebrow.

She shook her head, so briefly he wasn't positive he'd seen it.

Had Miss Betty gotten to her, too? Did Olivia have any idea what the old woman had planned for them?

"Mr. Clint! Mr. Clint!" Three young, identical blond-haired boys accompanied those boisterous voices. Clint immediately recognized them as Olivia's triplets.

And just when he'd thought things couldn't get any more complicated. Now it wasn't just about Olivia, it was about her kids, who were yammering on about something. "Come see! Come see!"

Every word out of their mouths seemed to be punctuated with an exclamation point. All three grabbed at his arms at once and started pulling his sleeves with all their might. Clint set his heels. They could tug all day and would not move him unless he wanted to be moved, but...

He turned his gaze on his foster mother, silently pleading with her to rescue him.

"Oh, go on. Don't be a spoilsport," Libby said with a laugh, waving him away.

Not what he wanted to hear. It was one thing to bow out of an obligation to the mother. But kids? How was he supposed to do that?

With a reluctant groan, he allowed the boys to lead him across the room. Maybe if he just followed them to whatever it was they wanted to show him, they'd leave him be and his problem would be solved. He wondered how quickly he could cut out if he saw an opportunity to do so.

It occurred to him that they might be guiding him toward their mother and that she'd put them up to accosting him, but Olivia had moved over to the punch table and was speaking to Carson and Ruby. The boys were clearly leading Clint toward the Sweetheart Wall.

"We made Valentine's cards in school," one of the boys said proudly. "We cut them out with scissors and everything."

"Yeah? That's…nice." And it had absolutely nothing to do with him. So why were the triplets so intent on showing him their valentines?

He looked from one to another, feeling stymied. He didn't know their names, and even if he did, he had no idea how he'd ever be able to tell them apart. They were especially daunting when they were all speaking at once.

"See?" another one of the boys said, pointing to a heart covered in childish print. "This one's mine. And that's Noah's, and that one over there is Caleb's."

As dark as the room was, Clint had to lean forward to read their cards, and what he saw blew him away.

Their notes were for their new daddy?

That was an odd thing for a kid to write, but one thing was for certain. It had nothing to do with him. Maybe Olivia already had a man on her horizon. Good for her. Clint hoped so for his own sake, so he could get out of this ridiculous matchmaking scheme unscathed.

"So does this mean you've got a new dad lined up to replace your old one?" he asked hopefully, then immediately wanted to kick himself. All three of the boys' smiles disappeared and sadness filled their gazes.

He was really, *really* not good with children. How insensitive could he be? He'd heard about Luke Kensington's accidental death a couple years back. These kids had been through a lot.

"Hey, I'm sorry," Clint said, crouching before them. He searched his mind for the right thing to say. "I'm sure you loved your daddy very much."

"He's in heaven," they said simultaneously. "With Jesus."

Poor kids. Clint didn't know about the "heaven" part of the equation, but he did know what it felt like to grow up without a father.

"My dad l—" Clint stumbled over his words. He'd been about to say *left*. Somehow he sensed that would make things worse for the boys. "—went away when I was about your age. So I know what it's like to grow up without a father."

"You're just like us," one of the boys said, excitement returning to his voice.

Not exactly.

Clint hadn't had a mother like Olivia to care for him. He'd ended up in the foster care system until he'd aged out. He'd been blessed to land at the Everharts' ranch near the end of his tenure, but his life had been anything but easy.

He nodded anyway. "Yeah. I guess I am."

"We're six."

"And we are in first grade. You came to our class to talk to us, remember?"

Now that he thought about it, he did remember seeing the triplets when he'd come to speak at the elementary school. It was part of his job as a trail guide to visit the kids' classes and encourage them to take wilderness tours. He didn't care for public speaking, but he did like getting paid to work in the mountains doing what he loved best, so he thought this was a decent compromise.

"We want to raise chickens and ducks, but our mom said we have to be more responsible first," one of the boys informed him.

"Yeah. Like we have to unload the dishwasher every night before dinner."

"And Mama makes us put our clean clothes away in our drawers."

The boys were animated and talking all over each other. Clint couldn't keep up and wasn't sure he wanted to. What was that they'd said about *chickens*?

"Hold on, guys," he said, lifting his hands in surrender. "I can't understand any of you when you're all talking at once. Slow down, and one at a time."

The sudden silence was more jarring than the chatter. Three sets of wide blue eyes stared at him, waiting for him to do—something. He had no idea what. At least they'd stopped pelting him with innocuous facts about their lives.

"You listen to your mama and do what you're told, and maybe you'll get those chickens someday. I think it's a good life lesson for boys to learn to be responsible for the care and feeding of living creatures."

"But we want them now." Clint noticed that the boy speaking had a bit of a cowlick in front.

"What's your name, son?"

"Noah."

Okay, so Noah was the one with the cowlick. Clint studied the other two for subtle differences. One had deeply carved dimples in his cheeks and the other did not. He pointed to the dimpled one. "And you?"

"Caleb."

"And I'm Levi." The boy grinned. He was missing his two front teeth.

So now Clint knew their names, and with effort could put the names with faces. He didn't know why it mattered. It wasn't as if he was going to see these kids again, never mind spend any time with them.

Which reminded him—according to Libby and Miss Betty, he was supposed to be chatting up the triplets' mother. He didn't want to give the old ladies any indication that he was conceding to their matchmaking in any way, shape or form, but he didn't know how else he was going to get rid of three clingy young boys besides guiding them back to Olivia.

"What do you say we go and find your mother?" he suggested. "She's probably wondering where you are."

"Will you ask her if we can have some chickens?" Caleb queried eagerly.

"And duckies?" Levi added.

Clint choked on a laugh. These kids were nothing if not persistent. "Well, I don't know about that. I think your mother ought to be the one making that decision."

"Making what decision?" A female voice sounded from behind his left shoulder.

He turned to find Olivia staring at him, her eyebrows raised and her hands perched on her hips. He didn't know why, but her demeanor made him feel she was scolding him.

He bristled. *He* hadn't done anything wrong. He was just trying to console her nosy kids. If she couldn't keep them corralled, he didn't know how she could expect him to do anything about it.

"Chickens," he replied, pressing his lips into a flat line. "Chickens and ducks, apparently."

"May I dare ask why you are speaking to my sons about chickens?"

"Hey, they were the ones who brought it up. I was just trying to be nice."

"Yes, well, thank you—I think. I apologize if they've been bothering you."

"No. They're fine. Really."

He didn't know why he'd said that. The kids *had* been bothering him—hadn't they? So why was he reassuring Olivia of just the opposite?

"Boys, leave poor Mr. Clint alone. Let's go grab a cookie before they're all gone." She pointed her sons toward the dessert table.

He watched her turn and walk away, herding her offspring with a deft hand, guiding them by the shoulders in the direction she wanted them to go.

He breathed a sigh of relief. At least that was over. He'd talked to her, right? That ought to soothe over any ruffled feathers with Libby and Miss Betty.

Only...

"Hey, Olivia. Wait up just a sec," he called. Even as he jogged toward her, he wondered at the wisdom of what he was about to do.

Olivia turned, her eyes widening in surprise. She looked as if he'd startled her. Maybe he had—but not as much as he was about to.

"You want to dance?"

Chapter Two

Olivia was certain she was gaping. Somehow she'd entered into an alternate universe, a twilight zone where Clint Daniels had just asked her to dance. She couldn't even begin to wrap her mind around it.

She'd never seen Clint dance. Ever. And even if he did dance, she was certain she would be the last woman on the planet he would choose as a partner, even with Miss Betty's blatant matchmaking.

And yet, there he was, standing in front of her, his hands casually jammed in the front pockets of fraying blue jeans as he waited for her reply. He must really be feeling the pressure. It was amazing what a simple valentine card could do to a man.

His gaze rapidly turned from questioning to impatient. "Well? Are you just going to leave me hanging here or are you going to dance with me?"

She opened her mouth but no words emerged. *Absolutely* she was not going to dance with him. It was totally out of the question. The triplets were bound to get the wrong impression, and in any case, she hadn't planned to hit the dance floor tonight. With anyone. But Clint was a formidable man to reject off-the-cuff.

"Please—don't feel obligated." There. That ought to do it. Let him off whatever hook he felt caught on. "I appreciate what Miss Betty was trying to do but, honestly, this really isn't necessary."

His brow lowered over stormy eyes, the green overshadowing the gold. "I don't feel obligated. Now do you want to dance with me or don't you?"

"The triplets—"

"Will be fine for the five minutes we're on the dance floor. We can both keep our eyes on them."

That wasn't what she'd been about to say. She didn't want the boys to leave the roundup tonight thinking they had a new daddy arriving in the near future, most especially not in the form of Clint Daniels. They had already hit him up once this evening, and goodness only knew what they'd been telling him. Whatever it was, she had to admit they'd been happy and animated.

And to her surprise, he'd been gentle with them. She wouldn't have expected a man like Clint to have a soft spot for children.

Hopefully, the boys hadn't mentioned anything in regard to her being on the lookout for a new husband. Their saying they wanted a new daddy could definitely be interpreted that way. She didn't want Clint to misconstrue anything her sons might have said, however innocently they'd meant it.

But maybe she was worried for nothing. All she'd picked up when she'd joined the conversation was some vague comment about chickens.

In hindsight, she should have headed off the triplets long before they'd shared anything personal about their lives—about *chickens*.

Oh, dear.

"Mama," Noah said, throwing his arms around her waist. The boys had realized she wasn't following them and had returned to her side. "I thought we were going to get cookies."

"We're hungry," Levi added, tugging on her arm.

"So am I." *Take a hint, Clint.*

"It's my fault she stopped," Clint said with a chuckle. "I asked your mother to dance, but she hasn't answered me yet." He crouched down to the triplets' level. "Let me in on a secret. Does your mama dance, boys?"

"Yes. Yes. She's a really good dancer," Caleb exclaimed.

"Yeah," Levi agreed. "She used to be a bal'rina when she was a little girl."

Clint chuckled. "Well, I don't know how much good her extensive ballet training will do with the Texas two-step, but I'm willing to give it a go. How about it, *Mama*? Shall we show your boys how it's done?"

"Dance, Mama. Dance." The boys echoed each other. All three were physically pushing and pulling her toward Clint. Her face had to be a flaming red. It was too crowded in the hall and the temperature was set too high.

"C'mon, Olivia. Let's give your boys something to talk about." He stood and extended his hand to her.

Her gaze swept from one eager young face to the next. She didn't want them to be talking about their mother and Clint sharing a dance, but how could she disappoint them when they looked at her that way?

"I—er—okay."

His hand, rough with calluses, engulfed hers, but that wasn't the half of it. This entire set of circumstances was swallowing her whole—and she knew who to blame for it. It was all Clint Daniels's fault.

"Cheap tactics," she muttered as he pulled her into his arms. "Using my boys to get me to agree to this. Low blow, if you ask me."

He leaned back to meet her gaze and then chuckled. "It worked, didn't it?"

"Don't encourage them."

"No worries." He pulled her closer so she had no choice except to rest her cheek on his shoulder. His hand easily spanned her waist. She was vibrantly aware of his nearness, the deep rhythm of his breath and the warm musk of his aftershave. His shoulder muscles rippled under her palm.

Everything she should *not* be noticing about him.

"Maybe you don't think so, but I'd rather not put ideas into their heads. It's bad enough that they discovered the valentine Miss Betty wrote that matched me up with you. Dancing? Only going to make it worse."

His chest rumbled with laughter. "So that's what it was. I was wondering why they chose to share the valentines they'd written with me."

"Exactly. If we're not careful, they'll be lobbying for you to be their new dad. I'm sure that wasn't what you had in mind when you showed up here tonight."

"Huh." He spun her around. "I think that may already have happened."

"What?" Olivia groaned.

Please, please, please let this not be happening.

He leaned down close to her ear. The music was so loud it was nearly impossible to carry on a conversation, even as close as they were—and they were close. Much *too* close for Olivia's liking. She couldn't seem to be able to still her racing pulse. She coached herself to breathe evenly, but all that did was cause her to get another good whiff of Clint's masculine scent. He must be wearing too much. It was making her giddy.

"It's just one dance. We'll pacify Miss Betty's penchant for matchmaking, and then we can walk away from each other and go on with our separate lives. Your boys will forget about me the second I'm gone. Sound good?"

Good was an understatement. She wasn't comfortable with the myriad of emotions coursing through her, and the sooner she got out of Clint's arms, the better.

As large as he was, and for someone who didn't dance much, Clint had a natural rhythm. He took the lead, but subtly and surprisingly gently. He twirled her around until her head was spinning. She refused to believe that her rapid breathing had anything to do with the man who held her in his arms.

Olivia sent up a silent prayer of thanksgiving when the music ended. Now, as Clint had said, they'd each go their own way, only slightly worse for the wear. She glanced around, looking for the boys.

"They're over there," Clint said, pointing to the far end of the room. It was a little disconcerting that it seemed as if he'd read her mind. "My foster mother, Libby, rounded them up and got them all cookies and punch while we were dancing."

It bothered Olivia that while Clint had been keeping his eyes on her children, she'd been completely lost in their dance. What must he think of her?

Heat rose to her cheeks. Again. She didn't fluster easily, and yet her interaction with Clint tonight had her thoughts going every which way including loose. She didn't like feeling scatterbrained.

It didn't help matters when he flashed a lady-killer grin and enveloped her hand in his.

"Don't worry. Libby has been a foster parent for years. She's great with kids."

"I can see that. And I wasn't worried." Olivia was mortified at her own conduct, maybe, but she wasn't worried about her children.

"There now, you see?" Libby said to Clint as they approached. "Aren't you glad you took my advice and asked Olivia to dance? You two made such a lovely couple out there. You were obviously enjoying yourselves."

Olivia gasped and then choked on her breath, feeling as if she'd just been hit behind the knees. It was a wonder she didn't fall over.

So *that* was the reason Clint had asked her to dance—and had been so intent on it. Not because he wanted to dance with her, or even, as he'd said, to pacify Miss Betty. Rather, he was favoring his foster mother's request.

Olivia's cheeks burned. She couldn't imagine why Clint's motivation mattered in the least. She'd been going to turn him down before the triplets got involved. And yet there it was—that small niggling feeling of rejection worming its way through her chest.

She was being ridiculous. This train had to stop *now*, before it jumped the tracks.

"Thanks for taking care of my sons." Happily, her voice had returned to normal, even if her knees were still shaking.

"It's absolutely been my pleasure," Libby responded with a kind, maternal smile. "You have some really wonderful boys right here. Three special blessings."

"Yes, they are." At least that was something they could all agree on.

"They've been telling me all about how their daddy used to take them camping and climbing, just like Clint."

Olivia's stomach lurched. The triplets had been only four years old at the time and she didn't know how much they remembered about Luke, who'd been a passionate outdoor enthusiast.

In fact, she'd lost Luke to a rock climbing accident, although she'd never shared that information with the triplets. Maybe when they were older and were in a better place to be able to understand. But for now she kept it silent and close to her heart.

"As it happens, my Clint here is a trail guide. He works full-time in the Deep Gulch Mountains teaching camping skills and wilderness survival tactics to young folks just like these handsome fellas. Your sons would love it."

Olivia nodded, more to be polite than really agreeing with Clint's foster mother. "I'm sure they would," she murmured courteously.

"Perfect," Libby exclaimed. "Clint can take your boys on a day trip, a beginner's challenge, and teach them all about wilderness safety. That would be fun, wouldn't it, Clint? Do you have a weekend opening where you can fit them in?"

Clint's wide-eyed gaze traveled from Olivia to Libby and back again. He looked as if he'd just swallowed a porcupine. Olivia felt exactly the same way and knew her expression probably mirrored his.

Unfortunately, the boys had been listening to the conversation. At Libby's suggestion, all three started cheering and chattering on about what they were going to learn when they went out with Mr. Clint.

Which was never going to happen. There was no way Olivia was going to allow her boys to go up into those mountains again, not even with a trail guide as experienced as she imagined Clint must be. Certainly not until they were much, *much* older, and even then Olivia knew she would have reservations. If Luke, who'd been a master rock climber, could meet his death climbing, who knew what could happen to three rambunctious six-year-olds?

There were too many variables.

Even if her fears didn't play into the equation, she wouldn't be inclined to let her children go anywhere with Clint. He might be a wonderful trail guide, but what did he know about kids? He'd been gentle and patient tonight, but she had no doubt her boys would wear him down in a flash. Olivia knew from experience what mischief they could get into in a short amount of time.

She shook her head. This had to stop now.

What was Libby thinking, offering his services without consulting him first? Clint rocked back on his heels and threaded his fingers through his hair. He was supposed to be done with Olivia Barlow, not planning to take her kids on an outing.

The dance was supposed to be the end of this fiasco. Now, apparently, it was just the beginning.

Even a beginner's challenge would be difficult for a six-year-old, never mind three of them. He might be able to keep their attention for a little while, but a day trip? Not so much. He imagined they'd be little terrors out there in the woods, running off in every direction at the drop of a hat. How on earth was he going to keep track of them and keep them reeled in? The very thought made him shudder.

But he could hardly beg off after Libby had made the suggestion. He pressed his lips together to keep from doing just that, afraid of what might come out of his mouth if he didn't.

"Thank you for offering, Libby," Olivia said, laying her hand on the woman's arm. "I appreciate you thinking of my boys. I'm sure a day trip with Clint would be fun for them, but I'm afraid we're going to have to pass this time."

Wait—what? Had she just turned Libby down?

Turned *him* down?

He bristled and stood an inch taller, squaring his shoulders and pressing forward on the balls of his feet.

She thought he couldn't do it, did she? She thought that he couldn't teach her boys how to enjoy the mountains, how to survive in the wilderness? Did she really believe that he couldn't keep them safe?

Who knew the Deep Gulch Mountains better than he did? Who else spent their days and many a night in the forest with only the light of the stars for a ceiling? He was far better than any boys' organizations that he knew of. His guided trail experiences were up close and personal, molded into whatever his clients most needed and wanted.

Pride flooded his chest, but it was a tender, guarded emotion. If he didn't watch out, she'd pop his ego like a sharp needle on a balloon.

"It will be good for them to learn new skills," he prodded. "Boys like being out in the open, and everyone needs a good survival course. Can't start too young."

Stop talking.

What was he doing? Digging himself into a hole? Probably, but he couldn't seem to stop the flow of his words.

"Be that as it may," Olivia said, lifting her chin and meeting his gaze square on. He wasn't intimidating her—not that he really wanted to, but she was calling his career into question. What did she expect? He wouldn't go down without a fight.

"What?" His emotional walls were in place. Impenetrable no matter what she said next.

"It's too soon."

That caught him off guard. What was too soon?

"Oh, Olivia, dear. I'm so sorry," Libby said, pulling her into a bear hug. "You're thinking of your Luke, aren't you? Well, of course you are. Clint and I are being completely insensitive, aren't we?"

Olivia's shoulders shook. Was she crying? Please—anything but that. Clint did not do well with a woman's tears.

Libby's gaze pleaded with him from over Olivia's

shoulder. But for what? What did she want him to do? Press forward? Back off? *He* didn't know what to do with Olivia's tears. He didn't even know what they were talking about.

Olivia stepped back and swiped her suspiciously wet cheeks with the palms of her hands.

"It's nothing against you," she said, motioning to Clint. "I'm sure you're a wonderful trail guide. It's just that—" Her sentence broke off as she looked at her boys. "Guys, why don't you go grab another cookie, huh?"

The boys squealed and took off toward the dessert table.

Clint silently waited for an explanation.

"I'm sure you remember that my husband passed away a couple of years ago. What you may not know is that he died in a freak rock climbing accident. They said one of his clamps gave way. And he was an expert. The triplets are not. I can't risk my boys getting hurt up there. They're completely inexperienced—and they're a handful during the best of times. One or another of them could easily slip away from you. Trust me, it happens all the time."

Clint nodded. "I get where you're coming from, but I assure you—they're totally safe with me. I won't let anything happen to them. Not on my watch."

Not like Clint's own father, who'd brought him up to the mountains and then just walked away. No. Nothing like that.

"I believe you," Olivia assured him. He didn't know whether she meant it or not, but her words were a balm to his bruised ego. "I just can't let them go with you. It's about me, not you."

That was that, then. It kind of sounded like a breakup line, but he would take what he could get. He thought that was the end of the subject, and he couldn't help but feel a little bit relieved. Going their separate ways—that was what he wanted, wasn't it? What they'd talked about? Agreed on?

Yet a small part of him wanted to prove to her that he was responsible, capable of leading her sons on a successful day trip. That they'd have fun and learn everything he had to teach them.

"I have a splendid idea," Libby said, jovially squeezing Olivia's shoulder.

Olivia smiled, but it was shaky at best. Her chin was still quivering.

"Why don't you go with them? It would do you good to get out and get a little fresh air, and that way you'll be right there to take care of the triplets and see that they don't come to any harm."

Clint's gaze widened. Come to any harm? Surely Libby didn't believe he couldn't handle three kids for one day.

"Isn't that a good idea, Clint, darling? Olivia accompanying you on the day trip?"

No. It was not a good idea. In fact, it was the worst idea he'd ever heard. What was he going to do with Olivia on the beginner's challenge? By default it would be targeted at six-year-olds. Surely she wouldn't be interested in a children's wilderness safety course.

And to top it off, he knew he'd get distracted. By her sparkling blue eyes. By the beautiful, full curve of her lips. By the rich oriental scent of her perfume.

Everything he'd discovered about her when they were dancing.

He wasn't marriage material, but he was a man, and he couldn't help but be attracted to a pretty woman. Olivia was definitely that and then some.

This whole thing was a disaster in the making.

"Maybe Olivia is right," he suggested, running a hand across the stubble on his jaw. "She's not ready to venture out yet. And the boys are still young. There's plenty of time for them to learn mountain skills."

"But we want to go now, Mr. Clint!"

He hadn't even seen the kids return, but there they were, and their expressions punched Clint right in the gut. He'd never seen such downcast features, complete with quivering lips and the onset of tears. These boys really wanted to spend time in the mountains. He got that. He felt the same way.

"Well…" he hedged. "What do you think, Olivia? We can take it as easy as you and the boys need to. It doesn't have to be a big production. We don't have to do the official beginner's challenge. I can tailor it to whatever your needs are. It might even be kind of fun."

Sure, if "fun" meant wrangling three overexcited youngsters for an entire day. He didn't think that qualified as a good time.

Olivia sighed and rubbed her fingers on the tense muscles at the nape of her neck. "I just don't know."

"You can trust Clint," Libby said, curling a hand in the crook of his elbow and patting his biceps.

"No, I know. Clint is the expert. So what exactly does this day trip entail?"

She was cracking, not that he could blame her.

How could she not give in, with Libby's gentle persuasion? In his experience, Libby could pretty much talk anyone into anything, himself included.

This whole taking-the-Barlows-on-a-day-trip thing being a case in point.

"We can take horses up Pine Meadow Trail. It's an easy ride and there are several places to stop and enjoy nature."

"It's just for a few hours, right?"

"Sure. Whatever you want. Give the boys a little taste of the mountains. Have a picnic."

She nibbled on her bottom lip and he couldn't look away. See? She was already distracting him, and they hadn't even started the beginner's challenge yet.

"Okay. But if we're doing this, I insist on bringing the picnic."

"I'm all for that," Clint agreed. "I can't cook a lick. Grab a package of hot dogs and we can roast them with a stick over a fire."

"And marshmallows?" Her eyes glinted, the first sign of interest she'd shown.

He chuckled and nodded. "Absolutely. Marshmallows, chocolate and graham crackers. What is a picnic in the mountains without s'mores?"

He pulled out his cell phone and opened his calendar. "I've got next Saturday available, or—"

His sentence was interrupted by a shouted exclamation and the murmur of the crowd.

"It's Robin Hood. He's here!"

Chapter Three

An icy finger of alarm skittered down Olivia's spine.

Robin Hood—the name of the thief who'd been casing Little Horn, rustling cattle and stealing supplies, only to turn around and fence them, making gifts to some of the less-fortunate, struggling ranchers in the area.

Hence the Robin Hood moniker—stealing from the rich to give to the poor.

He was here? At the Valentine Roundup?

He probably got a kick out of mingling with everyone, with no one the wiser as to his secret identity. It sounded cartoonish, except that it was not. It was frightening, especially to someone like Olivia.

With her tiny, struggling quarter horse ranch, she definitely fell into the latter category. She suspected Robin Hood would take one look at her and feel sorry for her, but that didn't stop her from worrying that she might be robbed next.

Who knew what the criminal was thinking—what he really wanted? His behavior was erratic at best and no one really knew what he was ultimately after. She couldn't afford to lose even a single horse in her already dwindling herd, never mind the trivial amount of equipment she owned.

But as much as the thought of losing any of her costly breeding stock horrified her, what concerned her the most was that the thief posed a possible threat to her children, however indirectly.

It was well-known in Little Horn that she was a widow. That made her vulnerable. An easy target. The thought that her triplets might not be safe on her own land frightened her more than she was willing to admit. She could hardly keep her squirrelly boys locked inside all day. They practically lived outside, running and playing and riding and wrestling. What if her triplets accidentally stumbled across Robin Hood when the thief was in the act of stealing something?

So far the guy hadn't been violent. He'd covered his tracks well. No one had had more than a glimpse of him, and as far as Olivia knew, Sheriff Lucy Benson hadn't had much success following whatever leads she had on him, nor had the Rustling Investigation Team that had been set up by the league for that purpose.

But a criminal was a criminal and in Olivia's mind, that made him dangerous. He had to know if he got caught he would be going to prison for his crimes. Put him in a corner and she was fearful that he'd come out biting.

Clint took her elbow and braced his palm against the small of her back. "Are you okay, Liv? You just turned white as a sheet."

She stared up at him, momentarily speechless. She didn't know whether she was more surprised by the fact that he was acting so compassionate toward her, or that he'd just used an unfamiliar nickname with her. No one in Little Horn called her *Liv*.

She shook her head. "It's Olivia," she corrected. "And I'm fine."

His brow lowered. "You're not fine. Let's get you seated on a chair and I'll go find you a bottle of water."

"No, really. You don't have to do that." What did he think? That she was Scarlett O'Hara, ready to pass out at the very thought of a crisis? Olivia had a lot more strength than he was giving her credit for. "I don't know about you, but I want to hear what's happening over there."

She gestured toward the Sweetheart Wall, where folks in the community appeared to be gathering—specifically, board members of the Lone Star Cowboy League and a small group of men and women who were unofficially investigating the crimes. They'd dubbed themselves "the posse." The name amused Olivia, though she knew Little Horn's sheriff, Lucy Benson, wasn't too happy to have inexperienced townspeople practically deputizing themselves.

"Fine," Clint said, following the direction of her gaze. "Have it your way. We'll find you a seat over there. But I'm still getting you a bottle of water." She thought she might have heard him mutter the words *stubborn woman* under his breath.

She considered herself entirely self-sufficient and it galled her to think he might be even the tiniest bit on target, but at least internally, she had to admit she *was* feeling a little light-headed—from the rush of adrenaline surging through her and concern for her farm. It had absolutely nothing to do with the man who wrapped his muscular arms around her as he guided her across the room, assuring himself as much as her that she didn't waver when she walked.

When they reached the Sweetheart Wall, she decided to ignore his dictatorial attitude in favor of a chair. Her own decision, not his. He had the bedside manner of an ogre, but she sensed that he meant well.

He led her to one of the nearest chairs, which were set up in a line against the wall near where everyone was gathered, mostly for use by elderly women and wallflowers. And widows, she supposed.

Clint waited until Olivia was seated before shifting to the side so he could take a glance at the missive that was causing all the commotion. He frowned and threaded his fingers through the hair curling around his collar. She'd been around him only for an hour but she already recognized the action as one he used when he was frustrated. Something he read had disturbed him.

"What is it?" The muscles in her shoulders and neck contracted painfully as she awaited his response. She held her breath.

"Robin Hood. He left a message on the wall in the guise of a valentine card."

"What's it say? Is it a threat?"

Clint swallowed and his Adam's apple bobbed. "Kind of, although it's not the sort of thing I would expect from a real criminal."

He cleared his throat and read:

"To all struggling ranchers: Funny how the Lone Star Cowboy League spends tons of money putting on a fancy event for themselves but doesn't seem to have enough to help those who are really in need.

"Jerks. Whatever. If they won't help, we will."

"That doesn't bode well for members of the Cowboy League." Olivia frowned.

"For any of us, really," Clint agreed, scrubbing a hand over his jaw. "I don't like the sound of it. I'm not a member of the league, but the Everharts are. I'm not convinced my presence on their land is enough to keep the Everharts from becoming a target. They don't have a large ranch, but it's relatively prosperous, and other comparable ranches have been hit. The thief might have started with the richest ranches in town, but they're working their way down. It's only a matter of time before they run out of league ranches and start robbing everyone else."

She reached for Clint's hand. He scowled at the Sweetheart Wall.

"We've got to find this guy," he growled. "And sooner rather than later."

"Guys," Olivia corrected, noting the worry lines creasing his face. He was clearly genuinely concerned about his foster parents. In Olivia's opinion, how a man treated his folks said a lot about him. That Libby and James were Clint's foster parents and not his biological ones made it even more touching.

"What?" He arched his blond eyebrows.

"The note says *we'll* help. Plural. Do you see what I'm saying? Clint, there's more than one thief out there." Her logical deduction did *not* make her feel any better. More thieves meant more opportunities for crimes to be committed. "Did the handwriting look familiar to you?"

The corner of Clint's jaw ticked. "Afraid not. It's typewritten."

Carson Thorn, the president of the Cowboy League, pressed his fingers to his lips and whistled shrilly over the uproar of the crowd. Folks immediately stopped talking and turned their attention to him.

"Can I get the remainder of the members of the league board and the investigation team over here? The rest of you can go back to the party and enjoy yourselves." He gestured for the band to strike up another tune. "No sense having this low-down criminal ruin the day for everyone. Don't worry, folks. The board and the sheriff's department are on it."

"And the posse," added thirty-something Amanda Jones with a frown.

Olivia chuckled under her breath at the name the group had given themselves. Right out of an old Western movie, where the sheriff "deputized" the good guys and they rode in to save the day.

In a sense, she supposed, the Lone Star Cowboy League was the good guys, providing much-needed support and services to struggling ranches around the area. They'd even developed special programs for the youth.

Her great-grandmother Lula May had been the only female founding member of the Little Horn chapter of the Lone Star Cowboy League, but Olivia hadn't been asked to join the investigatory group, possibly because her ranch was inconsequential compared to the ones that had been robbed, not to mention that she was a widow busy raising three young boys. She was struggling just to keep her twenty acres above water and even if she wanted to, which she didn't, she didn't have time to put into chasing local thieves.

Clint had just said he wasn't a member of the league, so he personally had no more at stake in catching the thieves than she did, but when their gazes locked and he arched a golden eyebrow, she knew he was thinking the same thing she was. They both wanted to know what was going on—firsthand.

The intentions of the thieves' movements were shifting, and it was anybody's guess where they were going next.

Clint reached for Olivia's hand and drew her to her feet, tucking her arm into the crook of his elbow. He glanced down, concern evident in his eyes. Maybe he still thought she was ready to swoon like an actress in an old-time film, but she was made of sterner stuff than that.

She smiled up at him. He nodded briefly and stepped into the rapidly forming group as if he belonged there. As if *they* belonged there.

"I've had enough of this nonsense," Byron McKay growled. "Lucy, when are you going to do your job and bring this thief to justice? I want him behind bars and prosecuted to the full extent of the law."

Byron, middle-aged and portly, was the vice president of the league and by far the richest land owner in the county. He was also the one who complained the loudest. Olivia supposed she couldn't completely blame him. He was the only rancher in the area to have been hit twice. Even so, his annoying blustering wasn't helping matters. Folks needed to remain calm and levelheaded if they were going to get anywhere with this.

"Thieves." Clint spoke up, his voice strong and steady. "Olivia was the one who first noticed this. Look here," he said, pointing to the typewritten missive. "These guys wrote 'we will,' not 'I will.' It appears we're looking for more than one criminal here."

She tightened her grip on Clint's forearm and he laid his hand over hers. As if one thief wasn't bad enough.

"There's something else in the wording of the letter that strikes me," Lucy said thoughtfully, curling her short blond hair behind her ears and peering at the thieves' card through her fringe of bangs. "The way it's written sounds…juvenile. Like teenagers. It's possible our profile is off and we need to adjust the age range of our thieves."

"I don't care how young they are," Byron bellowed, snorting like an angry bull. "Juvenile delinquents or hardened criminals. What difference does it make? It's your job to catch them and put them away for good."

Carson held up a hand. "We all want them caught, Byron. As you well know, we've got every rancher in town on high alert. Most of us have installed security cameras, and our wranglers are on the lookout for anything suspicious. Everyone is doing the best they can to find the culprits, both officially and off the books."

"Well, it's not enough."

That didn't seem fair. Olivia frowned. Sheriff Benson was working overtime on the case. She looked so drawn out and tired that Olivia felt sorry for her.

What more could Byron ask than her best effort? But then again, that was the way the McKays operated. Just because they had money they thought they were entitled to everything being handed to them on a platter.

Including, apparently, the Robin Hood—Hood*s*.

Only this time, it wasn't quite so simple.

Her gaze shifted to Byron's teenage fraternal twin sons, Gareth and Winston, expecting them to have the same snooty expressions on their faces as their father did. To her surprise, they looked embarrassed, maybe even a little angry that their dad was spouting off his mouth.

She didn't blame them. She'd be embarrassed, too, if Byron was her father. The man didn't know when to leave well enough alone. Hopefully, Byron's boys would grow up wiser and kinder than their father, taking a better path and becoming cooperative members of the Little Horn community.

To her credit, despite the personal attack on her capabilities as sheriff, Lucy ignored Byron's raging and focused on the typewritten missive. "It's too bad the note isn't handwritten," she remarked, intensely studying the veiled threat. "Someone might have recognized the print. As it is, I think we've made good strides today in further developing our working profile of the thief—er, thieves."

Carson nodded and folded his arms. "Right. So from the language of the missive, we're guessing they're youth. Teenagers, maybe?"

"Or they could be young adults," Olivia offered, thinking out loud.

Even an extended profile of the thieves was discouraging. She glanced around the room. There were probably close to a hundred teenagers in the room, and if she added everyone under thirty into the mix, that was a lot of people to investigate.

"The Robin Hoods are definitely old enough to drive a truck with a trailer attached and are familiar both with stock and ranch equipment," Lucy said. "There is no doubt that they grew up in the country, probably on a ranch and most likely in Little Horn. At least one of them is likely a male, since it would require a modicum of strength to move many of the stolen items. Based on everything else we've learned, I'd hazard a guess that we're looking for two or more young men."

"And one other thing," Olivia said, her breath catching as the realization dawned on her. The letter. The thieves had walked right into the grange and posted it to the wall and no one had even noticed. They weren't strangers, then. They were neighbors.

She shuddered. The thieves could be in the room with them at this very moment. She probably knew their parents.

"The note is pinned on the Sweetheart Wall," she said, raising her voice to be heard over the din.

Clint's brow lowered. "And?"

"And no one is allowed in the banquet hall unless they are a member of the league, or a member's guest." She gestured around the room. "Whoever put up this note is not only welcome at league functions, but has the ability to walk among us with no one the wiser. We aren't seeing them because they don't look out of place. They're one of us."

"So we need to narrow it down to league members," Lucy concluded. "We need to be especially aware of teens and young adults, although I don't want to rule out other possibilities at the present time."

The tone of the room immediately shifted. It was alarming that no one had noticed anyone posting the missive on the wall, because whoever it was was *here*—and belonged here.

People's gazes started shifting around the room as they examined and discarded possible culprits. Folks whispered among themselves. Pointed fingers and then shook their heads. Nodded and made quiet accusations.

Lucy held up her hands and turned to the secretary of the Little Horn branch of the Lone Star Cowboy League, a tall, gawky young redhead with an oversize orchid corsage on her wrist.

"Ingrid, I want a list of all league members and their families delivered to the station. We're closing in on the thieves. I can feel it in my bones."

"I agree," Carson said. "I think we're going to get these guys, especially because they're probably here tonight. We need to make a plan—question folks to see if anyone noticed a youngster putting a typewritten letter on the Sweetheart Wall—but we should organize our movements. Try not to stir up too much of a scene."

"Spread out and mingle. Don't rile people up. Perhaps someone saw something we can use," Lucy added.

"I hope so," Clint murmured in Olivia's ear.

"You'd better find *something* if you value your job," Byron said, a great deal louder than was necessary.

Clint met Olivia's gaze and briefly shook his head

at Byron's nonsense. Then he winked at her and his mouth curled up in an endearing crooked grin that sent her stomach tumbling. "Don't worry about your sons, Olivia. Byron's huffing aside, we're closing in on the thieves. Those Robin Hoods don't stand a chance now that I'm on board."

An hour ago she would have thought Clint was the most egotistical, narcissistic man ever if he'd made such a presumptuous statement. But now?

Now she saw a thoughtful, determined man who wouldn't stop until the thieves were behind bars. He might not be a superhero, but she was glad he was on her side.

Clint wasn't a member of the Lone Star Cowboy League, much less the Rustling Investigation Team, but he wanted these thieves caught as much as the next guy. More, even, now that he had Olivia on his arm. Who would have thought one hour with a woman could change his entire perspective?

How could he not be concerned about Olivia? She hadn't shared much with him, but she was clearly upset by the prospect of being robbed, and who could blame her, a woman alone with three young children? Her quarter horse farm might be one of the smaller and less flourishing ranches in Little Horn, but with no man around to protect them, she and her boys were especially vulnerable, ripe for criminal picking.

The targets the Robin Hoods were pursuing didn't have much rhyme or reason to them, even with the additional clue of the valentine card. At first they'd gone after the larger ranches and Byron had even been twice robbed. Some folks were pillars of the community. Others, like Byron, likely had made some enemies along the way.

Now the thieves were sometimes reversing their behavior, leaving gifts for those they considered needy instead of robbing. At best it was hit or miss and not typical criminal behavior at all, the medieval Robin Hood notwithstanding.

James and Libby, on whose property he lived, were also possible targets. Their ranch was also small but unlike Olivia's meager holdings, the Everharts were relatively prosperous. It was hard to say whether the thieves would think it was worth their time to target their ranch. Clint lived in a small cabin on the land. He didn't have any enemies that he knew about and he tried to be a good person, but he wasn't well-known in town. For all he knew, the Robin Hoods would use him as an excuse to rob the Everharts. Then again, his presence might be enough to deter any criminal activity.

Those thieves better hope they never had to mess with him, because he wasn't kidding around.

But what about the times he was away from the ranch? He spent many nights out in the Deep Gulch Mountains working as a trail guide and in search and rescue. He couldn't be everywhere at once.

And now he had Olivia and her boys to consider. What was he going to do about them? Odd that the Barlows hadn't even been on his radar before this evening, but if he'd learned one thing in his years as a foster child, it was that life could change in the blink of an eye.

As of now, he would do whatever he had to in order to get these thieves behind bars. On that one subject, he agreed with mouthy, arrogant Byron McKay, although Clint was willing to pitch in to catch the thieves and Byron expected everyone else to do the work for him. Entitlement was his middle name.

The man didn't know when to hold his peace. Even his kids were clearly tired of his ranting. Both Gareth and Winston looked as if they'd rather be anywhere but standing by their father. Gareth kept glancing at a small group of teenage girls who were giggling and gossiping. Winston just stared at his feet.

Clint's gaze zoomed in on the young men. In some ways they fit the profile of the thieves. They were male teenagers who knew their way around a ranch.

He considered bringing that point up to Lucy but then quickly discounted the notion as not worth mentioning. The McKays' ranch had already been robbed twice. It wasn't as if Byron's own sons would rob their father. Anyway, they were both too high in the instep to get their hands dirty.

There were so many teenage boys running around here that it would be impossible to narrow the field without interviewing each and every one of them, and even then, they might come up with nothing. Most of these young men had been born on ranches and worked cattle with their parents.

Jed Parker and Chris Cutter were fooling around with the sound equipment. It looked as if they might be sneakily rigging it up to play some of their music and taking over from the band. They could very well be the thieves the town was looking for.

Clint sighed. It seemed everyone was a suspect.

"What if they're right?" Carson asked, his expression grim. He leaned against the Sweetheart Wall and gestured at the missive. "About the Cowboy League, I mean. Are we doing enough to help struggling ranchers around here? We've got a few programs going, but we also throw events like the Valentine Roundup. Do you think anyone else in the area feels slighted besides these young men?"

"I know how much the league helped me after Luke's death," Olivia said, her voice both strong and thoughtful. Whatever her fears, she wasn't going to voice them to the team. Clint respected that. "If I recall correctly, y'all came out and helped me mend fences. And then several of you painted the barn for me one weekend."

She brushed a dark strand of hair behind her ear and continued. "I'm not the only one who has benefited from the league. Don't forget the programs and scholarships we offer to the young people. Future Ranchers, for one. The Stillwaters have done a lot with the teenagers in that program. Think about all the students we've helped over the years, and there's far more to that than monetary value. They feel our backing, the love and support the league members offer them."

The small group erupted in murmurs of agreement. Clint was impressed. The small-statured quarter horse breeder had turned out to be an impressive orator. Who would have thought?

"Tyler Grainger, for example. He was able to go to school and become a doctor because of the league. We have a real sense of community in Little Horn. The league was formed to help ranchers look after their own, and that's exactly what we do. My great-grandma Lula May would be proud."

As Clint recalled, Lula May was the only female

member of the original Cowboy League. That was back when women didn't usually have much of a say. She must have been one tough lady—much like her great-granddaughter.

"You think other ranchers feel that way? That the league is beneficial?" Carson asked, not sounding completely convinced. "Obviously someone doesn't."

"The missing town-limit sign," Lucy said, shaking her head. "'Welcome to Little Horn, Texas.' I get it now. That's what this is about. The message they're trying to send. They don't believe the league supports our community, or maybe they don't feel like they are being acknowledged in it."

"I can't speak for everyone, but I know all my friends and neighbors respect the league," Olivia assured Carson.

The rancher snorted in derision.

Clint clenched his fists. Somebody needed to give the man a good shaking, and at the moment he'd be happy to be the one to do it. Byron was vice president of the league, but that was just for show and so he could throw his weight around. If he started picking on Olivia, Clint would not apologize for his next actions.

"Folks ought to look after their own and not depend on the league to bail them out." Byron flung an arm around each of his sons' shoulders. They squirmed and looked miserable, and who could blame them? "Thanks to my own hard work, my sons will never rely on charity."

In a pig's eye.

Clint barely restrained himself from barking out a laugh. Byron McKay hadn't worked for a single thing he owned. He'd inherited every last bit of his wealth. If Gareth and Winston didn't have to worry about money, it was because their great-granddaddy had earned it for them, not because of anything their own father had done.

Olivia scoffed under her breath and Clint held back a grin. Apparently she was thinking the same thing. Byron was taking credit where credit was definitely not due. And he didn't have the league's best interest at heart. Clint doubted he believed at all in what the league stood for.

Maybe later Clint and Olivia could share a good laugh over the absurdity of it all, but now was not the time.

"Whoever these thieves are, they don't see things our way," he said, keeping his voice even. He still didn't know how he'd unexpectedly become invested in the league's business, seeing as he wasn't a member and didn't want to be. But suddenly it seemed very important that he be included in the investigation team's mission.

To keep Olivia safe. And the triplets. And Libby and James. And everyone else in Little Horn who was vulnerable. It didn't help matters that they were now looking at more than one thief, possibly even a whole band, of sorts. Robin Hood might be a more accurate name than any of them could have imagined when they'd originally branded the thieves with that moniker.

Then again, more thieves meant more chances for them to slip up. And if they were, in fact, local kids who were probably just having a lark, they would eventually make a mistake. It was a matter of when, not if.

Until then, he just had to make sure he kept the Everharts and the Barlows off the thieves' radar.

Clint gave Olivia's hand a reassuring squeeze. She wasn't alone in this. The league was here.

He was here. She was safe.

And he had some thieves to catch.

Chapter Four

She should have said no.

The triplets had been talking about nothing else for the entire week.

Mr. Clint this. Mr. Clint that.

How he'd promised to teach them all about ways to enjoy the Deep Gulch Mountains, where he worked as a guide. Saturday would be their first step to earning the coveted Junior Mountaineer badge that would make them the envy of all their friends. They'd have to work hard, he'd told them, to learn how to safely navigate the mountains so they could have fun without endangering themselves or others.

All Olivia could think of were sharp, hazardous rocks and steep, treacherous cliffs and how one misstep could be the difference between a man coming back to his family or never coming home at all.

Capital N. Capital O.

A simple two-letter word would have saved her from the throbbing headache that was currently pounding her temples to a pulp. She suspected it would get worse before it got better.

A rugged, blond, broad-shouldered headache.

How had she gotten herself into this?

Oh, well. It was too late to back out now. She'd just have to make the best of it and get this day over with. She was fairly certain Clint wasn't any more enthused about the outing than she was, but he'd graciously capitulated to his foster mother's wishes when she had offered.

If he could be gracious, so could Olivia. For one day, in any case.

With great reluctance, dragging her emotions if not her feet, she parked her truck at the foot of Pine Meadow. It was one of the lesser-used trailheads but the one nearest her farm, making it the most convenient for her.

Opening the trailer, she unloaded the four horses that would take them into the mountains. She'd purposely arrived a half hour early so she'd have plenty of time to tack up. She hoped Clint didn't notice the poor shape of her equipment. She'd had to sell most of her good saddles, and the boys were using what was left. It was especially embarrassing given that she owned a horse farm, but there it was. She'd done what she had to with the circumstances she'd been given. No sense complaining about it.

Having spent her entire life on a quarter horse farm, saddling the horses didn't require any mental effort on her part. It was second nature to her, which unfortunately left her mind free to wander—straight back to the reason she was here in the first place.

Clint Daniels.

After saddling the horses, she stepped back and monitored the boys as they bridled their mounts. The triplets were already good riders with excellent, natural seats. Their father used to say they were born on the back of a horse, and figuratively, anyway, they had been, learning to ride almost as soon as they could walk.

Olivia paused, waiting for the melancholy that sometimes rained upon her when she thought of Luke, but it didn't come. Instead, the memory flooded her with warmth and a note of joy. Grief was funny that way. She was glad that most of her memories of Luke now were happy ones.

The rumble of a truck's engine interrupted her thoughts. She glanced at her watch. Clint was early, with ten minutes to spare. So much for having time to mentally gear up before he arrived.

When he opened the door to his pickup, a frisky golden retriever barreled out before he did. The dog made straight for the triplets, wagging his tail and giving each of the boys doggy kisses while they squealed in delight. Despite her own anxiety, Olivia couldn't help but smile at her children's laughter. If she could bottle that sound she'd be a billionaire in no time.

"Pavarotti loves kids," Clint said as he clanked open the latch on the back of the trailer. "And he has the energy to match." He disappeared inside for a moment and reappeared leading a palomino quarter horse gelding. "Sometimes I feel kind of guilty that he has to live with a stodgy old bachelor like me."

Their gazes met as they shared a moment's amusement. Olivia's breath caught in her throat. A bachelor Clint might be, but the rugged cowboy was in

his physical prime and there was nothing dull or te-
dious about him.

Stodgy? She thought not.

He raised an eyebrow and she realized she'd been
staring at him. It was possible she'd even been gaping. Heat flamed her face and she cleared her throat.

"Pavarotti?" she asked, grasping on to the last non-
threatening statement he'd made. "Like the famous
tenor? So you're a closet opera lover?" She was jok-
ing, of course. *Clint* and *opera* were two completely
opposite ends of any spectrum she chose to measure
them by.

He shrugged and flashed a crooked grin that she
imagined sent every female's heart within a ten-mile
radius of him fluttering.

Not hers, of course. Her rapid pulse had nothing to
do with how good-looking he was or with the charm
behind his smile. Her response was merely the result
of being rattled by him when he caught her staring
at him as if she were a teenage girl crushing on the
most handsome boy in school.

What utter nonsense. She was a widow with three
active boys to take care of. She'd left *crushing* on
someone behind her long, long ago.

"You don't like opera?" His lips twitched.

She started to shake her head but then shrugged
instead. "Honestly? I wouldn't know. I've never even
listened to an opera, much less attended one."

"Don't knock it until you've tried it."

She struggled to wrap her mind around the star-
tling piece of information Clint had just offered her,
a glimpse into the inner workings of the man's mind.
It was nearly impossible for her to picture him, the

rugged and outdoorsy cowboy, all cleaned up for the opera and having a taste for fine music. She just couldn't see it. He was more suited for the back of a horse than the back of a limo.

Clint in a tux. Now there would be a picture for the *Little Horn Gazette*.

Actually, it kind of would be, now that she thought about it. An image of a knock-down, drag-out gorgeous Clint in a bow tie and tails filled her mind.

Realizing where her thoughts had gone, she shook her head and gave herself an inner scolding. She ought not judge the depth of his character by his hardy demeanor. So the man liked opera. Big deal.

"Is Pav a working dog?" She turned the conversation back to the golden retriever. "The kids said you visited their class and gave a presentation."

Clint's expression brightened and his hazel eyes turned a burnished gold. "Pav and I are a trained team. We're certified in search and rescue, although thankfully we haven't had to use our skills much in the Deep Gulch Mountains. Pav also accompanies me on all my guide tours. I've found my dog to be a great icebreaker. Loosens folks up."

Clint dropped his gaze to his boot and absently dug his toe in the dirt. Just before his eyes left hers, she thought she might have glimpsed just the hint of vulnerability, and it surprised her, leaving her to wonder if Pav helped *Clint* break the ice with the guests he guided on his tours.

He wasn't exactly a people person, and even if he was, she imagined his height, strength and rough exterior would be intimidating to many folks. From what she knew of him, he was a man who kept his own counsel. Not a big talker.

She suspected he'd rather roam the woods with just Pav for company, but a man had to make a living, even if that meant spending a day with a trio of rowdy youngsters and their reluctant mama.

Which would have made perfect sense, except that he'd refused her offer of payment, no matter how many times she'd asked. He told her not to worry about it, that he was doing this for Libby's benefit and to take money from Olivia wouldn't have been right. Pride made her insist on the matter, but Clint held his own. They were equally matched in the stubbornness department.

"First up, let's get the boys mounted on their horses." He approached Noah, who immediately and without reservation raised his arms to Clint, waiting to be picked up and plopped onto the well-worn saddle.

"Hey, cowboy." Clint smiled down at the boy. "It's Noah, right?"

Noah's grin spanned from ear to ear and he nodded enthusiastically.

If Olivia hadn't been gaping before, she was now. Few people on the planet could distinguish between the identical triplets, and Clint had been around them all of *once* before today. How had he done that? His power of perception impressed her.

"Looks like a bit of a jump to get into the saddle, yeah, little man?"

Much to Olivia's chagrin, Clint was absolutely correct in his observation. Heat rose to her face.

He'd noticed. It was probably blatantly obvious

that she'd recently had to sell off most of her newer pieces of tack, including most of her saddles. She could get by with what she had left, but they weren't pretty, nor were they sized for six-year-olds. As it was, she'd had to jimmy-rig the stirrups so they'd reach the boys' feet.

They'd grow into the saddles, she supposed, but it still hurt her heart that she couldn't provide them with all she wanted to give.

Clint linked his fingers and stooped by the side of the horse. "Grab on to the saddle horn and I'll boost you up," he told Noah.

"They usually use a bale of hay to mount their horses. They've been doing so since they were in preschool," she explained. "It does the trick. At least it will until their legs get a little bit longer."

When they were toddlers, Luke used to help them mount up. She remembered it as if it were yesterday. Luke would playfully grab their sons by the waist and toss them in the air one by one. Then he'd swing them around a couple times for good measure before depositing them safely in the saddle.

Maybe that's why she got so choked up when Noah reached so trustingly for Clint. He treated her sons like, as he'd called Noah, *little men*. He didn't talk down to them or disregard them. Pride beamed from three pairs of blue eyes as the boys settled onto their horses.

Clint rummaged around in the pocket of his jeans jacket and removed three silver whistles attached to strings, which he then looped over the boys' necks.

"Just one time," Olivia said, jumping in before the whistles could reach the triplets' mouths. She knew her boys well enough to know it would be too much temptation for them to wear whistles around their necks without having the opportunity to blow on them.

The area rang with the piercing sound of three whistles being blown simultaneously.

Clint chuckled. "I guess I should have thought about that. They're boys. Of course they'd want to try out their new whistles. Do you need a hand mounting?" He ran his palms down the front of his jeans.

She burst into laughter. "That's very sweet, but I may very well have more experience in the saddle than you do. I own a horse farm, remember?"

To prove her point, she lifted her foot into the stirrup and swung her other leg over, settling herself easily onto Cimarron's back.

"You're so tiny, and your mare is so large, I thought maybe you might use a bale of hay to mount, as well. I didn't mean to offend you."

"You didn't," she assured him.

Even before he'd explained himself she'd realized he wasn't trying to be a chauvinist. His offer was closer to chivalry. The thought of his large, capable hands spanning her waist as he lifted her into the saddle didn't offend her, but it certainly did...*something*. The flock of butterflies let loose in her stomach attested to that. But as long as she didn't acknowledge her emotions, they didn't count. Right?

"First, we're going to learn a little bit about wilderness safety," Clint said, adjusting the cinch on his saddle and mounting his gelding. He turned the palomino so he could speak directly to Olivia and the boys. "There's a nice meadow a few miles from here where we can stop and eat our picnic lunch. It has a fire pit and everything so we can…"

He paused and made eye contact with Olivia, lifting his brow in an unspoken question.

She nodded and patted one of the bulging saddlebags hanging across her mare's flanks. "All packed up and ready to go."

She might not have impressive tack to go with them, but her stock was top-of-the-line. Cimarron, a striking blood bay, was one of her leading broodmares. Olivia was proud of what she'd accomplished on her farm.

The boys' voices rose as they chattered in anticipation of the trail ride. Olivia ran through her checklist to make sure she hadn't missed anything.

She had packed hot dogs, buns, chips, graham crackers, chocolate bars and marshmallows. It was bound to be a messy meal, but no utensils were needed.

She planned to use the pocketknife she always carried to sharpen a few branches for them to skewer the hot dogs and marshmallows on and they would be in business.

She'd packed her sons' saddlebags with water bottles, a red-checked plastic tablecloth and a large package of wet wipes for sticky marshmallow hands.

It was the perfect picnic. But she wasn't trying to impress anyone. She wasn't.

"If all goes well," Clint continued, "then this afternoon I'll tell you all about the treasure hunt I've been on."

If the boys had been loud before, their volume increased a hundredfold when they heard the words *treasure hunt*. It was every little boy's dream to find buried treasure and dig for gold, although Olivia usually associated the words with pirates and not cowboys.

Clint led the small party down the trail and Olivia brought up the rear. Pav darted in and out of the forest, disappearing for minutes at a time, and then just when Olivia would start to get worried about him, she'd see a flash of yellow fur. Clint didn't appear concerned, nor did he even seem to notice, so Olivia assumed it was normal behavior for the golden retriever to be allowed to roam.

The triplets continued to babble excitedly as Clint pointed out signs of wildlife in the area and covered basic wilderness safety principles with them—always carry food, water, matches and a whistle. He promised he'd teach the boys how to use a compass but told them that carrying a GPS or smartphone for emergencies was even better. He admonished them to never wander off the trail. If they got lost and weren't sure which way to go, the very worst thing they could do was keep walking. Instead, he explained that they should find trees or bushes that offered some measure of shelter and stay put so the search and rescue emergency teams could track and find them.

Olivia had never thought of it that way. If she found herself lost in the woods, she would probably panic and walk around in circles. She was learning right along with the boys.

Clint was a wealth of information. He loosened up on the trail, looking completely at home in the saddle and in the environment. He was patient with the boys, even when they peppered him with questions. There was a depth to the man that she never would have imagined, and suddenly she realized she wanted to know more about Clint Daniels. Maybe Miss Betty had a point. Olivia would concede that much.

As if he had read her mind, he drew his horse up next to hers and settled into an easy walk.

"What about you, Olivia?"

Her heart fluttered under his scrutiny. There was no way he could have known she was thinking about him, but that didn't stop her from wanting to squirm in the saddle. She coughed. "What about me?"

"You look like you have questions."

Her cheeks burned and she knew her face must be a cherry red. If Clint's crooked grin was anything to go by, he had noticed her discomfiture.

"Nothing about wilderness survival," she admitted, not quite able to meet his gaze.

"I see. About me, then. Name, rank and serial number?"

"Something like that," she mumbled.

"My middle name is Aaron. I'm thirty-two years old. I feel cooped up and claustrophobic inside buildings and would rather sleep outdoors under the stars. My favorite go-to meal is a peanut butter and honey sandwich on white bread."

"That's all lovely." Her gaze locked with his and her breath left her lungs in a whoosh. Someone ought to put a warning label on those hazel eyes. They were hazardous to a woman's state of mind. "Now tell me something I don't know."

Her gaze showed genuine interest and her smile was full of natural curiosity, but unlike most women of his acquaintance, she didn't immediately turn the conversation around so that she was talking about herself. She'd actually asked about him, and she acted as if she really wanted to know.

But it made him uncomfortable that she waited for his response without speaking. For the first time in his life, he wished Olivia *was* what he considered a typical female. The silence stretched between them like a gaping chasm and the air snapped with tension.

And still she waited for him to answer.

He tried to pull his gaze away from her but couldn't. His pulse ratcheted. The sounds of the triplets talking and Pav barking faded into the background.

Olivia was so beautiful. Now he understood what people meant when they said someone took their breath away, because that was exactly what was happening to him right now.

He couldn't handle it, this painfully awkward pause. He had to say something to answer her question and break the silence between them. Something that would satisfy her curiosity and let him off the hook.

"Your boys are blessed to have you. I never had a home of my own." He waited for anger to fill him but it didn't come. Resentment was an emotion he could count on, something familiar for him to grasp on to. In its absence, he pressed forward. "I grew up in the foster care system. I always dreamed of having a mother who loved me."

Her gaze widened and flooded with compassion, and he immediately wanted to kick himself.

Now why had he gone and blurted out a fool thing like that? Sure, he'd been thumped around a bit by a few of his foster brothers and he'd gone hungry more than once, but how he'd grown up was nobody's business but his. Just after his sixteenth birthday he'd landed with the Everharts and had spent his last two years of foster care in a stable, loving, Christian home. It could have been worse. The last thing he wanted to do was evoke sympathy from her.

Or pity. Especially not pity. Life was a series of hard knocks. A man either battled them or he didn't.

Clint was a fighter.

"Look, forget I brought it up," he suggested, then trotted to the front of the line, not looking back. He could feel her eyes on him but refused to let that faze him—at least externally. Internally he was squirming like a mouse caught in a trap. When he reached a fork in the path, he guided them down a second, less-worn trail toward the meadow where they would have their picnic.

When they reached the open, grassy area, he quickly dismounted so he could help the boys off their horses, but they were clearly at home in a saddle, because they'd already slid off and had their mounts tied to a tree before he could even get his own horse tethered.

As he helped Olivia tote the saddlebags to the picnic area, he reviewed the triplets' names and features in his mind. Noah had the cowlick. Caleb had the dimples. And the third, by process of elimination, must be Levi. The boy without his two front teeth. Clint grinned when the boys took off chasing each other across the bluebonnet-dotted meadow.

He'd run in this very meadow as a child. He especially liked this area because it not only offered plentiful grass for the horses to graze on but also had a small creek running through it for the stock to get a cool drink.

It was his favorite spot to camp out in Deep Gulch and a very private and personal place to him. He'd built a fire pit for cooking, but until today he'd been the only one to use it. He couldn't imagine why he'd brought Olivia and her boys to his special place. He only knew it felt right at the time.

At least the tension in the air between him and Olivia had ceased. When she'd said she was going to bring a picnic, she meant it. A soft smile played on her lips as she unpacked all the goodies from the saddlebag.

Maybe, for a few hours, at least, he could wipe the stress lines from Olivia's brow. He knew the whole Robin Hood mess was getting to her. She hadn't said as much, but he guessed from the size of her ranch and the condition of her tack that she might be struggling. The last thing she needed was to have the threat of someone stealing from her—or worse, putting her or the triplets in danger—hanging over her head.

Together with Caleb and Levi, Clint built a fire in the pit, while Olivia and Noah went hunting for the perfect sticks on which to skewer their hot dogs and marshmallows.

When she and Noah returned, she wasted no time in setting up for the picnic. He spread a red-checked plastic tablecloth across the soft grass and she distributed bags of chips and bottles of water to each of them.

Together, they helped the boys spear their hot dogs onto sticks and cook them over an open flame. It was only afterward, when the kids had eaten and were off playing, that Clint and Olivia were finally able to settle down with their own meals and pick up where their conversation from earlier had left off. He'd hoped she would have forgotten it in the ensuing chaos and they would be able to move on to another subject, but the first words out of her mouth squashed those aspirations.

"It's nothing to be ashamed of, you know." Olivia folded her legs under her and leaned on a palm while Clint rested his forearm on his knee.

For a moment he considered pretending he didn't know what she was talking about, but in the end he just shrugged. "No—I know. I'm not ashamed. I'm just…angry."

She nodded, acknowledging his emotions without making him feel uncomfortable expressing them. He hadn't had this conversation with many people in his life and he could hardly believe he was having it now, except that for some reason Olivia was different. Maybe it was because she was a widow with three rambunctious children she had to raise on her own. She hadn't exactly walked an easy road, either.

"I can imagine," she murmured, her voice as soft and sweet as honey.

She tucked a dark curl behind her ear. Clint's gaze followed the movement, his fingers twitching with longing to pursue the same path.

"What happened to your parents?"

"My mom died in childbirth, having me." He clamped his jaw shut to control the emotions storming through him. He didn't like to talk about what happened to his mother and so he rarely did. "You wouldn't think, with as far as science has come, that women would still face the possibility of dying in childbirth, would you? We put men on the moon but we can't stop a woman from hemorrhaging to death."

He grunted and shook his head. He'd lived his whole life with that knowledge. The guilt. He had caused his mom to die. It had always bothered him believing that maybe his mother's death was the reason his father had eventually abandoned him.

Olivia reached for his forearm, silently giving him the strength to continue.

"I was about the age your triplets are when my dad brought me up here."

"To Deep Gulch?"

"Yes. Not far from this very spot, actually. It was my sixth birthday. We were supposed to be doing a treasure hunt. We were going to use his old-fashioned silver compass to find our way around. He gave me this little key." Clint reached for a gold chain underneath the collar of his shirt. Threaded onto it was a small silver key. "He said he'd hidden my gift inside a metal lockbox and it was up to me to use my mountaineering skills and riddle-solving abilities to find it."

If she hadn't been touching him he might have punched the air with his fist, just to have someplace for the bitterness and emotion to go. He shuddered in restraint.

"What was it?"

He scoffed. "There's the irony of it. I don't know. I never found the box, and not for the lack of trying. I've combed the land in and around Deep Gulch over and over again, but I've never managed to successfully put the clues together. It's just stupid that I can't let it go."

"Didn't your dad at least give you a hint?"

"My dad…" Clint paused and drew in a breath. "My *father* walked away from me that day. He completely abandoned me to the elements and didn't even leave me his compass to help me find my way out. If a couple of hikers hadn't run across my path and found me shivering and crying under a tree, who knows what might have happened?"

"I can't believe any man would just up and leave a child that way, especially his own son. What about bears and wolves and other wild animals? You must have been terrified."

"Believe it," he spat, yanking his arm away from her. It was impossible for him to be enraged and comforted at the same time.

He wanted to feel angry.

"Did they lock him up and throw away the key?"

The tone of her voice suggested she'd be glad to be the one to do it. She sounded every bit as irate as if she'd been in his place.

"I wish." Clint stared at a point just over Olivia's left shoulder, watching the horses munch the grass and the boys running in the field. "I don't know what happened to him. He was just—*gone*. Off the map gone. No one had a clue what happened to him. He had no living relatives. By the time I was old enough to really start looking, he was nowhere to be found."

Not that he'd tried very hard. Clint went back and forth between wanting to confront the man and shake the truth out of him and wanting to forget he ever had a father. Either way, he was damaged goods, of no use to anyone. His dad had made sure of that.

"You know what the worst part is?" Clint asked.

She raised an eyebrow and her full lips bowed into just the hint of a frown. "Tell me."

"I'm still looking for that stupid metal lockbox. I just can't seem to let it go. And all for what? A twenty-six-year-old kid's toy? It's not going to bring my dad back to me, and I'm not sure I'd want it to."

"Nor would it likely explain anything—at least anything important," Olivia mused.

"Exactly. And since the GPS wasn't available for civilian use back then, my clues are all based on riddles I don't understand, and the lay of the land."

"I would imagine the landscape has probably changed a lot in twenty-six years."

"No doubt. So you see, my quest is impossible." He knew bitterness was creeping into the tone of his voice but he couldn't help it.

"Nothing's impossible."

Her statement caught him off guard. He scoffed. "How do you figure?"

"With God," she finished. "Nothing is impossible with God. Have you prayed about it?"

Prayed? He hadn't even tried to talk to God. Not since he was a kid, when he'd prayed, begged, pleaded.

He'd learned his lesson—to depend on no one but himself. God had better things to do than fix his problems.

Yet Olivia sounded incredibly genuine in her faith. And that after the tragedy of becoming a young widow.

If her belief in God was what kept her going, he wasn't going to be the one to pop her bubble.

"Looks like your boys may be getting into a little mischief out there on those rocks." He gestured toward a mound of large, smooth, round boulders. They were high enough for a boy to enjoy climbing on but not so tall it was a long way to fall.

"Rocks?" Olivia jumped to her feet so fast she overturned her bottle of water onto the plastic tablecloth, but she didn't seem to notice. Her eyes had glazed over with sheer hysteria.

"How could you let them go near the rocks?"

Chapter Five

Olivia's heart slammed in her chest and adrenaline roared in her ears. Flashbacks of Luke's body dangling lifelessly from a harness off the side of a cliff burst through her mind and with that came the memories of all the trials she'd endured since then.

The newspaper clippings. The incessant telephone calls and emails from reporters hungry for a story. They'd refused to let her be alone to grieve. She'd had to identify and bury his body. Settle his affairs. Sort through his belongings. Raise the boys. And all on her own.

Because he'd slipped while rock climbing and hit his head on a jagged edge.

"Young men," she shouted as she ran toward them as fast as her legs would go. She waved her arms hysterically. "Get off those rocks before you hurt yourselves."

It was only then, through the thick haze of panic, that she realized the rocks the boys were playing on were merely large, round stones. At their highest they were only a few feet from the ground. Their playground equipment was higher than that.

And she looked like an idiot.

She skidded to a stop and Clint barreled into her, nearly taking her out. He wrapped his arms around her waist, tucked her head into his shoulder and used his momentum to turn them sideways. His quick thinking was all that kept them from landing in an inglorious heap.

Why had he followed her?

Her chest heaved and oxygen burned her lungs as she tried to regain her breath.

Clint slid his hands up to her shoulders, steadying her with his large, solid hands. He bent his head and his concerned gaze caught hers.

"Are you okay?" He frowned, scrutinizing her.

"I guess that depends on your definition of okay." Her cheeks blazed, half from exertion and half from sheer embarrassment.

The triplets joined them and Pav wound in and out of the group, barking with abandon. Olivia wrapped her arms around her three sons, reassuring herself that they were well and safe. "I just about had a heart attack."

"I can see that," Clint said.

"You must think I'm a complete ninny, getting rattled over nothing."

He shook his head. "It wasn't *nothing*. You looked like you were coming face-to-face with a grizzly bear."

"Or worse yet, my boys were." She scrubbed a hand down her face and then ruffled Levi's hair.

"I'm sure you think I'm overprotective, but even the thought of my boys climbing on the rocks…"

"Please don't put words in my mouth. Just because I don't understand doesn't mean I'm judging you." Light dawned in his eyes. "Oh, wow. I'm so sorry. I remember now. I—" His sentence skidded to a halt and he cleared his throat and nodded his head toward the triplets.

"You guys can play with Pav for five more minutes," Olivia told them. "Just don't go anywhere near the rocks."

The boys dashed off and Clint shifted Olivia so she was tucked under his arm, which he kept lightly draped around her shoulders as they walked in silence back to where they'd spread their picnic. For the first time in a long time, she felt safe, and she was grateful to the strong, quiet cowboy for giving her time to emotionally recover from the jarring experience.

Needing something to do with her hands, she focused her attention on gathering the empty bags and bottles and repacking the saddlebags.

"Your husband died in a rock climbing accident."

"Yes."

"It's perfectly natural that you would be concerned about your kids climbing on the stones. I should have thought before I spoke. I scared you unnecessarily."

Olivia couldn't imagine why Clint was trying to shift the blame to his shoulders. They hadn't been more than passing acquaintances before the Valentine Roundup. Now, thanks to three mischievous little boys and elderly, matchmaking Miss Betty Leland, their lives were suddenly and inexplicably intertwined.

Olivia had learned much about Clint today, about his past and what made him tick. Unfortunately, he'd had a glimpse of the worst and most private part of her, that underlying fear that something terrible was going to happen to her boys.

She trusted God. She *did*. So why wouldn't that niggling shred of apprehension go away? She was ashamed of her lack of faith and especially that Clint had witnessed it, however kind he was being about it now.

"Boys will be boys." She forced the corners of her lips upward but knew she missed the smile she'd been aiming for by a mile at least.

"And mamas will be mamas. Come on, Olivia. Don't be so hard on yourself."

"Says a man with no children."

She'd meant it as a joke but his hazel eyes clouded, darkening to a deep green before he looked away from her. "You're right. I wouldn't know."

She tried to backtrack but he spoke first.

"Hey, guys. Back to your horses now and let's get you mounted up. We need to get you home. It looks like it might rain."

The boys' faces fell. They'd been looking forward to spending the afternoon treasure hunting with Clint. Even Olivia had to admit she was intrigued by the possibility of a lockbox and the little silver key around Clint's neck.

He might be fishing for an excuse to leave but he was right. The once-clear blue sky had filled with menacing gray clouds. The five of them probably ought to return to the trailers before the sky opened up and drenched them.

As he'd done earlier, Clint crouched by each of the boys' horses and laced his fingers together, providing them with the extra leverage they needed to mount. By the time Olivia tied up the saddlebags and climbed on Cimarron, Clint was already mounted on his gelding.

"I'm sorry we won't have time to hunt for buried treasure today," Clint told the triplets. "But maybe next time we go out you can help me find the lockbox I've been looking for."

Next time?

There was going to be a next time?

Olivia didn't know whether to be pleased or distressed by Clint's pronouncement. The boys certainly enjoyed spending time in his company and they needed good, solid male role models in their lives.

On the other hand, Olivia was uncomfortable with the emotions Clint evoked in her. Or maybe that was *provoked.* Either way, she didn't know how to handle the way her stomach fluttered and her pulse raced whenever their eyes met.

She was *so* not ready to think about this.

"When I was little we used a compass to find our way around. These days, modern treasure hunting is called geocaching," Clint explained. "And you, little men, are called muggles."

"Muggles?" Olivia snickered. "Like in the Harry Potter books?"

"Exactly. Muggles are people who don't know anything about geocaching."

The triplets giggled, clearly delighted with their new moniker.

She narrowed her gaze on Clint. "You aren't going to call me a muggle, are you?"

He winked and flashed a toothy grin. "I wouldn't even think about it."

"Good. That's settled, then." She was relieved to see that he seemed to have forgiven her for speaking out of turn earlier. "Now tell us more about these modern-day treasure hunting expeditions."

"Right." He seemed reluctant to break his gaze away from her, but after a moment he released his breath and trotted to the front of the line, turning his gelding back the way they'd come. He allowed the horse to have its head and twisted halfway in the saddle, bracing his palm on the gelding's flank so he could continue the conversation, or lecture, or whatever it was. He was a good teacher with interesting stories, and the boys were paying close attention to him.

"Believe it or not, geocaching is quite popular all over the world. There are entire chapters of geocachers. Basically, someone hides capsules, which are modern-day treasure chests, and the information on where to find them is posted online. Folks split into teams and use a GPS to try and find the treasure. When they find it, they don't take it. Instead, they add proof that they've been there and leave the capsule for others to find."

"That's no fun," Caleb said, scratching his head. "How come no one wants to keep the gold coins and silver cups and everything?"

Clint burst into laughter. "Sorry, bud. There isn't any gold buried in those capsules. But I'll let you in on a little secret about another treasure, one that's hidden right here in Deep Gulch."

He told the triplets about the treasure he'd been seeking, leaving out the part about his dad abandoning him.

"Cool. A real treasure!" Noah exclaimed.

"Is there gold?" Levi asked.

"No. No gold. But I suspect there's a toy in there that a six-year-old boy would like. Or three boys."

The triplets were getting more excited by the moment. Clint caught Olivia's eye and they shared amused smiles.

"But first I've got to figure out the riddle I was given. Maybe you muggles can help me with that."

"We're good at riddles, aren't we, Mama?" Noah asked proudly.

"You sure are." Olivia's curiosity was piqued, as well. Clint hadn't said much about the riddle when they'd been speaking about it earlier.

"Okay, so here it is. 'Three grows into one. Joy watches over.'"

"That's it?" Olivia asked. "Three what?"

Clint groaned and lifted his hat by the brim, brushing his shirtsleeve over his forehead. "I wish I knew. I've ridden through this area hundreds of times over the years but I've never been able to figure it out."

It was thoughtful of Clint to bring the triplets in on his private treasure hunt, especially as personal as this was to him. Perhaps he saw a little bit of himself in the boys. She knew what it took for him to open up the way he was, but she hoped he knew what he was signing up for. Once her sons wrapped their minds around the idea of finding real treasure, especially a toy interesting to a six-year-old boy, they were unlikely to let it go.

The five of them reached the trailers and Clint helped her unsaddle the horses and run a brush over them.

"We'll have to set up another day trip," he told her. "Next time we'll focus on the treasure hunting. The muggles really seemed enthused about it."

"You have no idea." She snorted and shook her head. "All three dressed up as pirates for the church harvest festival last year."

"I can wear an eye patch." Clint squinted one eye shut. "Aargh, me mateys."

She couldn't help but smile at the thought of the rugged cowboy playing the part of a pirate. She liked this lighthearted side of him. And she liked that he seemed to genuinely care about her sons.

"Would you like to come back to the farm for a cup of freshly ground coffee?" she asked.

"That sounds wonderful, but you don't have to do that for me."

"I'd like to. I really appreciate all you've done for my sons today. You won't let me pay you, so it's the least I can do." She leaned down and scratched Pav's ears.

Clint hesitated and she could see the vacillation in his eyes. He was on the fence and it was up to her to knock him over onto her side.

"I've got chocolate chip banana bread. Homemade and baked this morning."

He groaned in delight and patted his lean stomach. "You're hitting my weak spot. Banana bread is my favorite."

"You'll come, then?"

He nodded. "I'll follow you back to your farm."

All during the twenty minute drive to Barlow Acres she debated the wisdom of inviting Clint back to her place. She didn't want him to misread her intentions or think she was interested in him in more than a platonic way. She had good reason to be concerned, since her own heart was sending out mixed signals and she didn't know how well she'd concealed her jumble of emotions.

But as she'd told him, she owed him for his generosity in spending the day with her sons, especially because he'd refused to take any money for it. The least she could do was serve the man a cup of coffee and a slice of banana bread. What harm could there be in that?

She pulled into her long gravel driveway and backed the trailer to the barn door while Clint pulled his truck in front of the ranch-style house.

She was unloading Cimarron when the boys scrambled up to her, each excitedly shouting over the other in an effort to be heard.

"Mama, we got chickens!"

"And saddles!"

"Duckies!"

What on earth?

She held up her hands to quiet the overagitated trio, but they ignored her, chattering at the top of their lungs and tugging at her arms and shirt, begging her to follow them to see what they'd discovered.

She didn't know what they thought they'd seen, but she let them pull her around to the back of the barn, laughing at their sheer joy and enthusiasm. They'd probably seen a flock of geese and mistaken them for chickens, but she supposed it wouldn't hurt for her to play along with them for a moment.

When they rounded the corner of the barn shock slammed the breath from her lungs. She clamped a hand over her mouth to muffle her cry.

An enclosure had been hastily constructed out of a coil of chicken wire, and inside were three hens and a half dozen fuzzy ducklings. Three newer-looking children's saddles were slung over the split rail of a nearby corral fence.

She spotted a piece of paper that had been rolled up and stuffed into one of the holes in the poultry netting.

Her heart in her throat and her pulse pounding with adrenaline, she unrolled the missive.

"For your boys."

She tried to pull in a breath and choked on it.

She'd been targeted. And it was personal.

"Robin Hood."

Clint was exiting his vehicle when he heard what he thought was a distressed cry coming from somewhere around the back of Olivia's barn. A woman's muffled shriek.

Pav's ears pricked and he let out a low growl.

Olivia.

With his heart beating out of his chest, Clint took off at a dead run toward where he believed the sound had come from. All kinds of scenarios entered his mind, everything from Olivia twisting her ankle in a gopher hole to finding herself face-to-face with a rattlesnake.

Lord, protect her.

Clint wasn't a praying man, but if it was a rattle-snake, he could very well be too late to help her. He wasn't convinced God had his back, but Olivia had faith, and right now Clint could use all the help he could get.

His boots were kicking up a trail of dust from the gravel as he rounded the corner of the barn. He immediately scanned the area for danger. He didn't see anything out of the ordinary, but when his eyes landed on Olivia, he knew something was wrong.

She was gaping and her face was as white as a sheet.

He didn't think. He just acted, sprinting to her side and wrapping his arms around her, loaning her his strength and a shoulder to lean on. She gripped his shirt with both fists and buried her head in the cotton material.

Her whole body quivered under his touch. Was she sobbing? Probably, but she wasn't making a sound. Clint tightened his embrace. He still hadn't a clue what the problem was and it tore at his heart that all he could do to help her was hold her as she cried.

Whatever was wrong with her, it didn't appear to be a physical threat to her or the boys, at least not one that he could see. And while he didn't wish harm on her, at least with a snake or a bear he would have known what to do.

A crying woman? Not so much.

Without a reason to act, there wasn't anything more he could do for her except hold her and keep a watchful eye on the triplets, who were gathered around their chicken coop.

Clint recalled how at the Valentine Roundup the boys had chattered their heads off about how much they wanted to raise chickens. He was glad the boys had gotten their wish. It was nice to see them so happy. He could tell how excited they were about it.

Good for them—although it looked as if they needed a little more help constructing a sturdy coop. He wondered if the boys had been left without supervision to build it themselves. It looked like something a six-year-old would make. A good, stout Texas wind would send the haphazardly placed coil of chicken wire flying.

"I see your boys got their chickens," he said aloud, hoping he could take Olivia's mind off whatever was bothering her. But the moment he said the words, she shuddered and responded with a distressed murmur.

He reached for her shoulders and bent his head so he could see the expression on her face. He was surprised to find that the tears he'd expected to see in her eyes were noticeably absent.

She'd been trembling, not sobbing.

"Olivia?"

She pressed her lips together for a moment as if to contain her emotions. When she finally spoke, her voice came out dry and cracked. "Robin Hood."

"What?" Clint wasn't sure he'd heard her correctly, or maybe it was taking him an extra long beat for the information to set in.

"The chickens. The Robin H-Hoods."

No wonder she was quivering. "The thieves were here? Did you see them? What did they take? Some of your chickens?" He didn't mean to overwhelm her with questions, but his mind went into overdrive and a protective instinct welled in his chest, overpowering all the other emotions he was feeling.

Just the thought that Olivia and the boys might be in harm's way was enough to make his pulse pound in his ears. There was no way he was going to let something happen to them. Not while he was around to stop it.

Her jaw ticked with strain. "I haven't done an inventory, obviously, but I don't believe they've taken anything. They gifted us. The chickens. Those saddles." She pointed at the corral, where three polished leather kids' saddles were slung over a wooden split-rail fence.

That explained why the chicken coop was strung so haphazardly. The thieves had done it in a rush so as not to be discovered.

Except in this case, they weren't acting like thieves—they were acting as benefactors. Rob from the rich and give to the poor. They'd certainly earned their nickname with this special delivery.

"And there was this." She shoved a rolled piece of paper toward Clint's chest. He took the note with one hand and brushed his other palm across her cheek, framing her jaw. With his thumb, he gently tilted her chin up so she could meet his gaze.

"You're not alone here." It was all he could think of to say. As strong and resilient as she'd been until this moment, he didn't expect the tears that welled up in her eyes. She squeezed them closed in a clear but vain attempt to rein in her emotions, and a single teardrop rolled down her cheek.

Her gaze darted to the triplets. "I'm worried about how they are going to deal with all this. They've already taken on too much responsibility for me as it is. They consider themselves the men in the house. What will they do if they discover we might be in danger? That's just way too much of a burden for my six-year-olds to handle."

"You're right about that, but I think you'd be surprised at the way a guy's mind works—even with the little fellows. We like to feel like we're protecting our loved ones. Every little boy wants to be his mama's superhero."

"Yes, but—"

Clint slid his hand down her arm and grasped her hand, giving it a reassuring squeeze. Her fingers felt ice-cold against the warmth of his palm.

"I don't believe you're in any danger from the thieves. Think about it. From the profile the investigation team has developed to date, it's looking more and more like they're only a couple of kids. Probably out on a lark. They stole the town sign. That's hardly something an adult would do—or a dangerous criminal. And while they've stolen quite a few high-ticket items and will likely be in a world of trouble once they're caught, they haven't threatened anyone, nor have they given us any reason to believe they would. No one has seen more than a glimpse of them. The second they think anyone is on to them, they take off running."

Clint nodded toward the chicken coop. "They left gifts for you. Why would they do that if they meant to frighten you or steal from you?"

Her shoulders slumped. "Read the note."

He unrolled the paper and glanced at its contents. "This just confirms what I already suspected. These fellows believe they are helping you out. We need to call the sheriff and let her know about this."

Olivia's eyes widened for a moment and then she nodded.

He fished his cell phone out of the holder clipped to his belt and punched in Sheriff Benson's number.

"Lucy, it's Clint Daniels. We have a situation here over at Olivia Barlow's farm. It appears the Robin Hood thieves visited while we were out today."

Lucy released a labored sigh. "What did they steal this time?"

"Oh, no. They didn't take anything. They left poultry and saddles for the triplets. That's all I know about for sure. We haven't really looked around yet."

"Hang tight. I'll be right over. I'd prefer you leave things just as they are until I get there."

Clint agreed, punched the End button and then placed his cell in its belt holder.

"Lucy is on her way over," he informed Olivia, whose expression remained unchanged. "Hopefully, we'll find some clues as to why they chose you and your sons as recipients of their gifts."

Her jaw ticked. "I hate even thinking about it. It's worse than if they'd stolen from me."

"What? How do you figure?"

"I've let her down." Olivia's face crumpled.

"Who? Lucy?" Clint frowned in concentration. Somewhere along the way he'd lost track of where the conversation had gone. Just as he did when he was performing search and rescue work, he backtracked to the last place he'd seen clear evidence of a path.

The Robin Hoods. Stealing from the rich and giving to the poor. Was that the problem? Olivia was embarrassed that the thieves had placed her squarely in the latter category?

"My great-grandmother," Olivia answered belatedly. "Lula May Barlow."

"Why do you think you've let her down? I don't believe that, by the way," he added.

"She was an amazing woman. So strong and brave. She came out West as a mail-order bride at age nineteen and married Frank Barlow, a widower with two sons, and then had two children of her own with him. She was widowed at age twenty-eight, but even before then, Frank's health had declined. She'd been running Barlow Acres on her own for years. She had an amazing gift with horses, and news of her breeding program spread far and wide. People came from states over to buy her horses."

"She sounds like quite a lady."

"She was—and she was spectacularly successful in a time and place where being a woman was a complete disadvantage. She never let that deter her for a second." Olivia pulled in a long breath. "Not only that, but she was the only female member of Little Horn's original Lone Star Cowboy League. She held her own with the best of them.

"That's the reason I kept my maiden name after I married Luke. And why the triplets carry the name Barlow, as well. Barlow Acres is my legacy, and some day I hope it will be my sons', too. My dream has always been to pass the farm to them when they reach adulthood. But with the way things are going now, there won't be a horse farm to hand down to them. I've lost a great deal of acreage already, not to mention breeding stock."

"I think you're just like your grandmother."

Olivia's gaze met his and her pupils dilated, turning her eyes a midnight blue. She sniffed and shook her head in disbelief before she turned her head away, looking in the general direction of the children and the chicken coop. Her expression became thoughtful and distant. He could tell she was wrestling with her memories.

Didn't she realize how strong and brave she was? It took a special kind of woman to raise triplet boys on her own. They were good boys, too. Obedient and respectful, if a little bit rowdy at times.

She frowned. "I'm nothing like Lula May."

"I beg to differ." Clint struggled to keep his tone firm yet gentle and to find the right words with which to encourage her. "Olivia, look at me."

He was determined to clear up any misappropriated guilt and shame she might be feeling, and encourage her to see how valuable she was. He wanted her to see herself as he saw her.

Reluctantly, she turned her gaze to him, and her eyes carried such despondency that it gutted him clear through.

"Lady, you don't give yourself nearly enough credit."

She started to rebuff him but he shook his head and continued before she could speak. "When I look at you, I see a woman every bit as brave and determined as Lula May. You have a different set of circumstances, but they are at least as much of a trial as anything Lula May might have had to endure. You've had some setbacks, but you keep fighting. Your boys see that, Olivia. They have a good, stable, loving home to grow up in, and you're the reason why."

The kind of home Clint had longed for in his youth but had never had. He only wished Olivia could see his perspective. Then she'd know how special she was. Levi, Noah and Caleb were blessed to have her as a mother.

Clint wanted to tell her all that, but before he was able to express how he was feeling, he heard a vehicle door slam shut. The sheriff was here. He'd hesitated too long. The time for words had passed.

He was impressed by how quickly Olivia gathered herself. She brushed her hair back behind her ears, squared her shoulders and lifted her chin. "Boys, why don't you go inside and wash up? With soap. Make sure you scrub your faces and under your fingernails."

The triplets groaned collectively.

"But we want to watch the chickens and duckies some more," Levi wailed.

"I named my chicken Bob," Noah added.

Even with all the strain she was under, Olivia laughed. Clint was glad to see her smile.

"I think the big chickens are all girls, sweetheart."

"Eww," Caleb said. The other boys joined him in expressing their distaste.

Clint chuckled under his breath. The triplets might not appreciate the opposite gender now, but there would come a time when they would feel differently. As adults they might find, as he was, that they would be fighting their attraction to a woman.

"One of the ducklings might grow into a fine mallard," he reminded them. That appeared to mollify them. They raced toward the house, each one trying to run faster than the others to reach the front porch first. Pav followed, barking, until Clint whistled him back.

Lucy approached, her notepad already in hand. She pushed back her short blond bangs.

"Sorry we have to meet under these circumstances. What have we got here?"

If Lucy was curious as to why Clint was hanging out at Olivia's horse farm, she gave no indication of it, for which he was grateful.

They'd already been spotted together dancing at the Valentine Roundup. The last thing Olivia needed right now was to be the center of idle gossip from folks with too much time on their hands. Like most small towns, Little Horn had an active gossip mill. It worked nearly as fast as the prayer chain did. Speculation about a romance between Clint and Olivia would be sure to spark interest and spread like a Texas grass fire.

Romance? Where had that notion come from?

Clint mentally shook himself and returned his attention to the present moment and Lucy's questions.

"As far as I can tell, we're the recipients of those three saddles over there and the chickens in the coop," Olivia said.

"There was a note," Clint added, handing the missive to Lucy. "I don't think there's any doubt that we're dealing with the same thieves who've been sweeping the area lately. It fits the pattern, or what we know of it, anyway."

"The saddles make sense," Lucy said, "but do you have any idea why the suspects would have left you chickens? Are they included in what this note is referring to? Is it specific to your boys?"

"It is," Olivia confirmed, crossing her arms and rubbing her palms against her skin as if a sudden cool breeze had emerged. "To be honest with you, I'm kind of creeped out by the whole thing. It's all so—*personal*."

She shivered again and Clint wrapped his arm around her. Hang the gossips. Olivia needed his support right now.

"If it makes you feel any better, this is probably the one and only time you'll encounter them," Lucy assured her. "The only ranch to be hit twice was the McKays', and that's probably due to their affluence."

And, Clint thought, possibly their arrogance.

Olivia winced and scrubbed a hand down her face. "I'm not afraid, exactly. But you have to admit it's unnerving—whoever the thieves are, they somehow knew how much my boys wanted chickens and ducklings."

Lucy scribbled this new information in her notebook. "That's not common knowledge?"

"No, not really." Olivia paused and pursed her lips. "Oh, wait. I remember now. I was talking to Amelia Klondike last week in church. I think I may have made an off-the-cuff remark about the triplets' obsession with chickens." Her gaze widened on Lucy. "Does that mean the thieves were worshipping at *church* with us last Sunday?"

"Could be," the sheriff acknowledged. She walked around the coop, examining the area thoroughly for signs of disturbance.

"But not necessarily," Clint was quick to add. "The

boys were yammering on about chickens at the Valentine Roundup, too. Somebody might have heard them then."

Lucy wrote that information in her notebook. "I'd like you to keep your eye out for anything suspicious. With what the Rustling Investigation Team has put together so far, we believe the suspects are two or more local teenagers or young adults. They're holding a grudge against Little Horn in general and the Lone Star Cowboy League in particular. The sign was stolen."

"Professional thieves wouldn't be interested in swiping a sign. But wouldn't teenagers likely just vandalize it?" Clint asked.

"Hard to say. They may have been trying to send us a message. It's just one of dozens of pieces of the puzzle right now." She paused thoughtfully and rifled through her notebook. "Due to the evidence we've gathered, we believe at least one of the thieves is sweet on Maddy Coles."

Lucy flashed them the page that contained Maddy Coles's picture. "Do you know her? Any connections you might be able to give me are highly appreciated."

Clint frowned, his mind grasping for something that was just beyond his reach. Something about the picture looked vaguely familiar to him. Not the red barn—that was similar or identical to dozens in the region. Not the girl. Her face didn't ring a bell with him at all. But something…

Lucy was in the process of cataloging the saddles and the various poultry in her notebook when a call came in on her cell phone.

She shrugged apologetically. "I'm sorry. I have to

take this. Excuse me for a moment," she said, stepping away to speak to whomever was on the other end of the line. From the gravity in her tone, Clint guessed it couldn't be good. Poor Lucy had really had to go above and beyond recently.

·"Do you think the thieves struck twice in one day? And in broad daylight? Have they ever done that before?"

Absently, he rubbed the knots of tense muscles in her shoulders. "They've been getting braver, which also means they're getting more and more careless. It's only a matter of time before someone catches them in the act or spots them running away and recognizes them. Most of the ranchers have security cameras now. The whole town is on high alert and the sheriff is just a phone call away."

Olivia squeezed his biceps. "You're only saying that to reassure me."

Heat crept up his neck. "Just making an observation."

He did want to reassure her, and he fully intended to protect her and the boys. But he didn't want to step on her toes in the process or make her question her own abilities. She was a proud, independent woman and well able to take care of herself and the triplets.

"Well, I'm thankful you were here with me today just the same. I don't know what I would have done if I'd been alone when all this went down."

"You would have been fine." He hoped she didn't hear how scratchy and tight his voice had become. His heart swelled and lodged right in his throat and it was a wonder he could breathe, much less speak. He could hear the difference in his tone. He felt as if he'd just swallowed a handful of gravel. "You're more courageous than you give yourself credit for."

She chuckled, but it was a dry sound devoid of humor. "I suppose you're right about that. If I see a spider and I'm the only one around, you can bet I'll be standing on the nearest table screeching at the top of my lungs. But woe to the arachnid that dares to come near my children. I am quite efficient with a flyswatter and insect spray."

"See? There's a mama tiger inside you just waiting to be let out of her cage."

Ugh. What was it about Olivia that made a man open his mouth and insert both feet? She might very well interpret his words as flirtatious, which made him come off as an uncompassionate lout. Now was not the time for levity.

Fortunately, he was saved from having to dig an even deeper hole in the conversation when Lucy came back to join them, her eyebrows scrunched together over her eyes.

"I'm afraid I have to go."

"Everything all right?" Clint asked.

"It appears the Robin Hoods have been especially generous today."

Olivia frowned. "They visited another ranch."

Lucy confirmed Olivia's statement with a brief nod. "The Donners. Apparently the thieves came sometime during the night and left a hay baler in one of their back fields. They only just discovered it this afternoon."

A *hay baler*? How did a thief leave such a large piece of farm equipment in a field without anyone noticing? They would have had to make a great deal of noise. And yet once again, the Robin Hoods had gotten in and out without being caught.

"Go," Olivia urged. "A hay baler trumps chickens and saddles. We'll be fine."

"Please leave everything right where you found it as much as possible."

"Will do."

As the sheriff walked away, Clint studied Olivia's ashen face. Her jaw was set and determination flared in her eyes, but Clint thought "fine" might be pushing it.

"I'll be right back," he told Olivia before turning to jog after Lucy.

He caught up to the sheriff just as she reached her marked SUV. Her gaze widened in surprise. "What's up?"

Clint dragged in a breath. "I'm not a member of the Lone Star Cowboy League and I don't want to be. But the posse? You can count me in."

"I prefer the name Rustling Investigation Team."

"You can call it Prince John's Henchmen for all I care. But I'm sure you'll agree this has gone on long enough. They're scaring the locals." Clint stopped just short of mentioning the most pressing reason he was concerned: Olivia and the triplets. "I want those young men caught, and I'm guessing you can use all the help you can get. Plus, I've got Pav," he said, gesturing toward the golden retriever at his left heel. "He's not a police dog but he's trained in search and rescue. Who knows if he might help us at some point?"

Lucy stared at him for a long moment before answering. "Agreed. You're in. Just don't go all vigilante on me. Promise?"

He jerked his head in concurrence. He'd color within the lines. For now. But if the Robin Hoods dared get near any of the people he cared about again, the posse or Rustling Investigation Team or the entire town Lone Star Cowboy League would be the least of those thieves' concerns.

Chapter Six

Olivia poured batter onto the griddle and watched for the telltale bubbles that would indicate she should flip the pancakes. It was Barlow tradition for as far back as she could remember to have pancakes, scrambled eggs and bacon on Sunday mornings after church. Before church they were usually in too much of a rush to eat more than toaster pastries with a glass of milk.

She had to admit she hadn't paid as close attention to the service as she should have. Her mind kept wandering back to the evening before. It had all been rather odd, and it wasn't just about the Robin Hoods.

Clint had surprised her. He'd hovered around for a good three hours after Lucy had left. Olivia hadn't been entirely certain he was going to leave at all. He'd gratefully accepted the cup of coffee she had offered and made himself at home at her kitchen table. Then it was two cups, and then three, and still he lingered.

When he'd made no move to leave, she'd seen no other choice than to invite him to stay for dinner.

Awkward.

Or at least, it should have been. She hadn't entertained a man at the table since Luke had passed away. But Clint had made it comfortable for her. For a man who spent most of his time alone, he'd been surprisingly easy to talk to.

Not only that, but he'd offered to set the table, he'd entertained the triplets with stories from his guide trips and had regaled them with what he'd learned in search and rescue training. He'd even insisted on rinsing the dishes and putting them in the dishwasher.

She was used to Luke, who'd never once helped with household chores. He'd insisted on doing *guy* chores. He'd mowed the lawn. Taken the trash to the curb once a week. Fixed the occasional plumbing problems.

But laundry? Dishes? Never happened.

Then suddenly Olivia had had an outdoorsy cowboy at her sink with a frilly apron tied around his waist, quite literally whistling while he worked. She'd felt as if she was in some kind of twisted, backward fairy tale.

With his height and broad shoulders he'd been a complete juxtaposition to the feminine surroundings, which had only highlighted his masculinity. The dish towel he'd slung over his shoulder was embroidered with colorful wildflowers, and yet no matter how out of his element he appeared, he couldn't have looked more rugged if he'd tried. Every single movement had enhanced his…*maleness*, for lack of a better term. Olivia had found her gaze straying to him again and again, no matter how hard she'd tried not to look at him.

When, at the triplets' insistence, he'd tucked them

into bed for the night, there had been a deep tenderness and reverence in his words and actions that had astounded her and had made her heart well with longing. He'd read them a story in a soft, calming voice and had listened to their sweet little prayers, even joining them in a heartfelt "Amen." Then he'd tucked their blankets under their chins as if it was something he did on a regular basis.

When she'd thanked him for his effort, he'd simply and quietly told her it was something he'd always wanted to do—and that he was glad he'd had the opportunity to do it once in his life. Since he was an orphan himself, he had no brothers and sisters and thus no chance to become an uncle to nephews or nieces.

She'd noticed he had said nothing about marriage and a family of his own. He bared his heart completely when he interacted with her sons. But Olivia suspected he didn't see that part of himself, the goodness in his heart, and he didn't realize the wonderful gifts that God had given him.

Maybe that was why the Lord had placed her and the boys in Clint's life—to open his eyes to the possibilities of his future.

She only hoped the triplets didn't get too attached to Clint in the process. He would tire of the novelty soon enough and move on. Or the thieves would be caught and Clint would no longer have a reason to stick around. He was only here in the first place because of some misguided sense of chivalry and an obligation he felt he owed to his foster mother. Olivia knew better than to read any more into the situation than what was right there on the surface. That was a good way to get hurt—or for her sons to get hurt, and that would even be worse.

She'd just finished pulling the last crispy strip of bacon out of the frying pan when the doorbell rang. Expecting the sheriff, she wiped her hands on her apron and went to open the door. Lucy would want to finish investigating the area around the crime scene, if she could really call it that. It was strange to think of a crime scene involving giving and not taking, but it was all pieces of the same puzzle.

"Come on in," she said as she swung the door open. "I have breakfast on if you'd like to—"

Her sentence slammed to a halt when she realized it wasn't Lucy on the other side of her door.

It was Clint, hat in one hand, a fresh-picked bouquet of Texas wildflowers in the other and a thousand-watt smile on his face. The man could have been in a toothpaste commercial.

"Am I going to get in trouble if I admit that I purposefully timed my visit to coincide with what I hoped was mealtime?" He thrust the flowers forward. "These grow up next to my house. I thought you might like 'em."

"They're lovely. And you're welcome to eat with us. Hotcakes, bacon and eggs. Scrambled. I don't take special orders. It's too complicated."

He laughed. "Scrambled is fine."

Wait a second. Why was he here again? It couldn't be as simple an explanation as that he was hungry. So what was up with him?

"Mr. Clint! Mr. Clint!" the boys exclaimed, leaving their seats at the table and running to circle Clint's waist.

He laughed and patted their shoulders.

"Boys, you aren't finished eating," Olivia reminded them. "Back to your seats, now."

She followed Clint in and loaded his plate with food as she considered how to politely ask him what in the world he was doing at her house on a Sunday afternoon.

"All's quiet on the western front?" he asked before forking eggs into his mouth.

Oh. So that was it. He was checking up on her to make sure the thieves hadn't made a reappearance. That explained a lot, but it didn't clarify the ripple of disappointment that washed over her that he wasn't here for another reason.

He washed his eggs down with a long swig of coffee. "I'll take your silence as a yes."

"No. Yes. I mean, we're fine. No more visits from the thieves. You could have called, you know, and saved yourself a trip over here." She knew he had her number. They'd spoken on the phone regarding the day trip they'd taken yesterday.

"I could have," he agreed, a sly half smile creeping up his face. "But where's the fun in that?"

She'd just taken a sip of coffee, and she gasped, both because of his words and at the amusement warming the gold flecks in his eyes.

The scalding liquid went down the wrong pipe.

She choked. Reached for her throat. Coughed. Choked again. Tears stung her eyes.

Clint was immediately by her side, supporting her and keeping her upright while he gently patted her back. Even with his help, it was at least a good solid minute before air returned to her lungs.

"I know I leave women breathless, but I have to admit this is the first time I've ever made a lady choke."

His words sent her into another coughing fit because she was laughing so hard. She swiped at the tears in her eyes with the palm of one hand. "You're killing me here."

"Well, now, that would really be a first for me." He flashed her another cheesy grin and his deep rumble of laughter joined hers. "Killing a woman with laughter. Charting into unknown territory."

She was feeling a little loopy, and as far as maintaining any dignity and decorum went, well, that ship had sailed long ago. She'd snorted her coffee right in front of him. Not exactly ladylike.

Clint reached for a piece of his bacon and had it gone in two bites. "Okay, all kidding aside, I spent the evening thinking about the pathetic attempt at a quasi coop the thieves set up for the boys' birds. Clearly the Robin Hoods were in a rush not to be seen. A good, stout wind would blow that coil away, and the poultry along with it. You're going to need something a great deal more substantial to hold your chickens long term."

The triplets immediately latched on to Clint's words and perked right up. It warmed Olivia's heart to see how happy and excited they were, which made it all the more painful for her to have to be the voice of reason. She wished she didn't have to be the one to burst the boys' bubbles and it made her angrier than ever at the Robin Hood thieves for the way they'd disrupted her family's lives.

They thought they were helping?

It was bad enough that they'd deign to visit her farm at all, but to put ideas in her sons' heads...

If—no, *when*—they caught the thieves, Olivia had an earful ready for them. Little Horn's sheriff's department and the Lone Star Cowboy League would be the least of their worries. She'd make the crooks thankful that they were behind bars and out of her reach.

"Lucy said we're not supposed to touch anything," she reminded them, cringing when the boys' faces fell. Maybe someday she could pursue raising chickens with her sons, but now was not the time. As Clint had rightly pointed out, she didn't even have a workable chicken coop and had neither the knowledge nor the materials to make one.

Even an economic hutch would cost money she didn't have. Besides, the birds didn't really belong to them.

Clint grinned and winked at the triplets. "Yes, but we don't want those ducklings running away. I think we have a legitimate reason to keep them around. They're evidence, aren't they?"

Olivia frowned. "I suppose so, but I don't—"

"Have to worry about a thing," Clint finished for her. "I happened to have some extra two-by-fours and some plywood lying around the ranch. I thought the boys and I could build a nice, sturdy hutch for the birds while we're waiting for the sheriff to arrive."

"Today?" Olivia's stomach fluttered. Clint threw around words like *we* and *us* without thinking about it. He'd completely and seamlessly inserted himself into the family, and the triplets were eating it up, exclaiming in delight and crawling all over their "Mr.

Clint" as if they were monkeys and he was a piece of playground equipment.

Rather than ignoring them or freezing up over the boys' roughhousing, Clint laughed and encouraged them, wrestling them to the carpet until he had all three pinned and squealing in his grasp.

That, Olivia thought, was possibly what her sons needed the most now that Luke was gone—a man's perspective and attention. It would never have occurred to her to roll around on the floor with them. Board games were more her style.

She'd been about to order the boys back to their seats to finish eating, but then she would have missed the joy on all three of their faces as Clint wrestled with them. She hadn't seen the boys appear so happy and carefree since…well, it had been a while.

In that moment, she decided it was worth opening her dismally lean pocketbook for this one occasion, even if she had to dig into her meager savings to foot the materials for the chicken hutch.

"I'm sure the boys would love working with you on the coop. What do I owe you?" She reached for her purse and tunneled inside for her wallet. She didn't have much cash, but she could write him a check.

"*Owe* me?" His hazel eyes widened in confusion and his blond brows disappeared under his hairline.

"For the materials," she clarified and then wondered if she ought to offer him something for his time, as well. She didn't know if he was turning away work to help them out.

Clint didn't often attend the Little Horn Community Church, other than with his foster parents on Christmas and Easter. She thought perhaps that was because he was busy guiding weekend outings. Certainly he had better things to do than hang out at her house on a Sunday afternoon.

"You think I'm asking you to pay me?" He sounded genuinely offended and Olivia took a step backward.

"Materials don't come cheap."

"Like I said, I had extra wood lying around that probably would have gone to waste otherwise. I'm happy to be able to find a good use for it. Consider it a gift."

Now he sounded as if he was trying to persuade her to let him build the hutch. "Let me do this for you—for the boys," he stammered, his cheeks reddening under her scrutiny.

Pride welled in her chest but the more practical side of her pushed it aside. When he put it that way, how could she refuse? The boys were over the moon, not just because they were getting a hutch to hold their beloved chickens, but because Mr. Clint was going to help them build it. It was the best of both worlds.

"Do you have a spare sheet of paper?" He sank into his chair and pushed his empty plate aside. "Let me sketch out my general ideas real quick and then you can add any observations you'd like to make."

She laughed and shook her head, holding her palms up in surrender. "I can tell you right now that I'm not going to be of any help in designing a chicken coop. That is *so* out of my skill set." She reached for a notebook from the nearest kitchen drawer, pushed it toward him, and then passed him the only pencil she could find.

"No special requests?" he joked. "Easter egg laying room? A covered deck with a chicken swing?"

He started to draw and then lifted the pencil. "This is the first time I've worked with a superhero pencil, at least that I can remember, anyway."

"It comes with the territory."

"Your mama is way cool," Clint told the boys, but his glittering gaze was on her.

Her cheeks warmed and his grin widened.

He finished the drawing and slid it across the table for Olivia to see. "It's a modest hutch," he explained, "but your ducklings will have their own separate housing and your hens will be safe to nest and provide you with many more meals like this one." He gestured to his empty plate.

She had to admit she liked the idea of having fresh eggs every morning, and taking care of the chickens would serve to teach her sons responsibility. It would be a great learning experience for them, caring for their very own live animals. They helped with the horses now, but the chickens would give them a sense of proprietorship they now lacked.

"Does this work for you?" Clint asked.

"It's perfect." She couldn't think of a single modification she would make. He was the chicken-coop-making expert here. And speaking of "way cool" people, the way Olivia saw it, Clint was right up there with the best of them. A superhero without a cape. She was certain her boys thought so, too.

It wasn't long before they were all caught up in the excitement and experience of building the hutch. The fresh, early spring Texas air was a balmy seventy degrees and they didn't even have to wear jackets while they worked.

Olivia was less than useless with a hammer and

nails, so she threw herself into hauling boards and beams from Clint's truck to the area where they were working. The triplets made the process a little more difficult than it could have been when they insisted on "helping" to carry the wood.

She could only imagine how trying it must be to let each of the boys have a turn measuring the wood, using a circular saw to make precise cuts and hammering nails into the beams. Clint never once lost his patience with the triplets. He didn't even come close. In fact, he was having at least as good a time as they were.

Before long they had the framework built and Olivia helped them string up and staple new chicken wire around the hutch—fencing that was still in its original packaging. From the looks of it, she had her doubts that *all* the materials had been lying around Clint's ranch as he'd said they were. She suspected he'd bought at least part, if not all, of them for this specific project, but she couldn't exactly call him out on it without appearing rude or ungrateful.

Especially when she felt quite the opposite. She wanted him to know just how very much she appreciated what he was doing for her—er, for her sons. But before she could even form the words, the sound of a car's tires crunching across the gravel driveway drew her attention.

The sheriff, no doubt. Gratitude would have to wait until later, when they were alone.

While Clint and the boys worked on what Clint said was a little surprise for Olivia, she went to greet her.

"How did it go with the Donners?" she asked as

Lucy exited her SUV. "Is everyone all right over there?"

Lucy nodded and sighed in exhaustion. Olivia could only imagine how much extra time she'd had to put in on this investigation. The woman frowned and stress lines appeared at the corners of her mouth.

"The Donners were another ranch on the receiving end of this case. I hated to have to take the hay baler into evidence, but it couldn't be helped. It's too bad, though. That equipment would have made their harvest much easier on them. In that regard the Robin Hoods are right."

"You took the baler into evidence?" Olivia hadn't wanted the Robin Hoods to visit her with their "gifts," and she knew that whatever she'd been given had been stolen from someone else, but it hadn't occurred to her that Lucy would immediately have to take the chickens away.

She'd known the sheriff would want to investigate the site of the crime, of course, but not confiscate the chickens. Her boys were going to be so disappointed at the loss of their beloved poultry, especially after having worked all day with Clint building the new hutch.

It couldn't be helped, Olivia supposed, but that knowledge didn't make it any easier. Sadness flooded through her and she bit back frustrated tears.

It wasn't in her budget, but she could buy more chickens. The only problem was they wouldn't be *these* chickens. She knew her boys had already set their hearts on these particular birds and there would be no reasoning with them.

"Did you discover anything else out of the ordinary after I left yesterday?" Lucy asked as they rounded the corner of the barn. "Did the thieves leave anything else or take anything that you noticed?"

"No. Just the saddles and the birds."

"Hey, Olivia. Come look what the boys made for the ducklings." He tipped his hat, acknowledging the sheriff. "Lucy. Good to see you again."

"That's a mighty fine-looking hutch," Lucy said as her gaze skimmed over the new chicken coop. "Did you build all this in one day?"

It was a rhetorical question, since she had been standing in that very spot yesterday and the hutch had not been there—not to mention the fact that she was perfectly aware that the chickens were a recent development.

"Thanks to my three little helpers here," Clint said. "And Olivia, of course. I couldn't have done it without her."

Olivia snorted. As if she'd been useful in any way. Yeah. Carrying boards. Her greatest achievement.

He shifted his gaze toward her and raised an eyebrow. "Do you want to come see what the boys have been working on? It's pretty cool."

Both Olivia and Lucy moved toward the hutch, and the boys stepped back so the ladies could take a look at their project. Olivia crouched down to watch the ducklings playing in a shallow pond of water. Clint had fashioned a waterfall and a tiny slide for them to go down and to Olivia's astonishment, the little ducklings were lining up to take turns sliding down the poultry-sized playground equipment.

"That's amazing," she exclaimed, realizing there was a great deal she didn't know about the care and feeding of chickens and ducks. She'd need to read up on that. Thankfully there was the internet and how-to videos.

"You moved the chickens out of the coop the thieves left them in?" Lucy asked, her gaze skimming over the scrunched-up coil of chicken wire that wouldn't have contained the chickens, much less the ducklings, for any longer than it had.

But still—Lucy had told them not to touch anything, and here they'd gone and moved all the poultry.

Clint lifted his hat and wiped his sleeve across his glistening forehead. "If I hadn't moved them, they would have escaped. The ducklings were already crawling through gaps in the coil. I didn't want your evidence running away."

"It's a good thing for you that I checked the area yesterday. Otherwise, you'd be guilty of disturbing a crime scene and I'd have to toss you in the can."

"Don't worry. I double-checked for tracks and other disturbances before I trod in the grass with my big feet."

Lucy laughed. "I'm sure you did. Excuse me a moment while I go have a look at the saddles and the area around them. One can only hope I find something useful over there. A footprint. Their names written in the dirt. You know—evidence."

Olivia waited until Lucy was out of earshot before she whispered, "I thought we were going to be in trouble for a moment there."

He shrugged. "I carefully examined the area before I went in after the poultry. I promise you there wasn't anything to find. Tracking is my day job, remember? Lucy trusts my expertise. Don't you?"

"Of course." Olivia didn't have to think about the answer to that question. She trusted his tracking expertise, but it was far more than that.

She trusted *him*. Implicitly.

"And I can't tell you enough how much I appreciate what you've done for me and my boys today."

He seemed to inflate. His shoulders broadened and he stood a good inch taller. "It's my pleasure, Olivia. Spending time with you and the kids has been—"

Lucy returned and he didn't get to finish his sentence, leaving Olivia to wonder what he'd been about to say. Spending time with them had been—*what*?

"I'm afraid I have to confiscate the evidence," Lucy said, frowning regretfully. "This is the hardest part of my job. However misguided these Robin Hoods are, they are leaving thoughtful gifts, things people really need. I hate to be the one who has to take stuff away. I know your boys could really use those new saddles."

The triplets hadn't shown much interest in the saddles, and they didn't appear to be fazed by the fact that Lucy was about to take them away. To a six-year-old, a saddle was a saddle. Who cared if it was new or used?

But the chickens and the ducklings…

Olivia closed her eyes and braced for the worst.

Even at a distance, Clint saw the shudder that ran through Olivia when she closed her eyes. He frowned and swept his gaze to Lucy and back. When they'd been speaking only minutes before, Olivia's face had been flushed with color, a lovely rose. But now her skin looked white and peaked.

Was she angry? He'd only been trying to help her and the boys by building them a hutch, and he'd been careful in releasing the poultry from the makeshift coop. He hadn't interfered with the investigation. He hadn't disturbed any evidence because there was no evidence to disturb. Even the sheriff had said so.

They wouldn't get fingerprints off a chicken.

Olivia inhaled deeply and opened her eyes, frowning when she glanced in his direction.

So she *was* angry with him. He blew out a frustrated breath.

Olivia followed at Lucy's shoulder as she approached the hutch. "I'm sorry about your new saddles, boys, but I'm afraid I'm going to have to take them away with me. The people that left the saddles and chickens for you are—bad guys. Do you understand?"

Lucy paused, looking hopefully from Clint to Olivia. Clint felt for her. How did a person explain the concept of a Robin Hood–type thief to a six-year-old, especially one—rather, three—who'd just been gifted with exactly what they'd been wishing and hoping for?

"The thing is," Olivia interjected, "these saddles belong to some other little boys or girls. I'm sure they're missing them right now."

The boys nodded solemnly, taking the news with remarkable composure. But then suddenly Noah's eyes widened and his gaze turned to the birds.

"You aren't going to take our chickens, are you?"

Feeling as if he'd been struck by a bolt of lightning, all the pieces of the puzzle came tumbling together for Clint in the blink of an eye. Lucy's pinched mouth, Olivia's frown and now the three weeping boys.

The sheriff was about to confiscate the triplets' poultry. And it was going to break their little hearts.

"Surely that's not necessary." He offered what he hoped was the voice of reason.

Lucy shrugged. "I'm afraid it can't be helped. Those saddles—"

"I wasn't talking about the saddles. We all understand why you have to confiscate those. I was referring to the chickens. And the ducklings. You can certainly take the crumpled coil with you if you think it will be of any use to you, but we just built a good, solid hutch to contain the birds. Surely there's no need to move them."

Lucy's gaze widened on him, but it was Olivia's expression that made sparks electrify every one of Clint's nerve endings. She was looking at him as if he was the superhero on the pencil she'd lent him earlier. His chest filled with warmth.

"I hadn't gotten as far as considering what to do with the chickens," Lucy admitted. "I'm not sure there's a protocol for stolen poultry."

"But they're stolen merchandise," Olivia said.

Surprised, Clint flashed his gaze to her. She was once again frowning, and who could blame her? He admired her honesty, even if she pushed it to the point of causing herself and the boys pain, but there had to be another way around this dilemma, a way everyone would win.

"Do you have any reports of stolen chickens?" he asked.

Lucy shook her head and pushed her blond bangs

out of her eyes with the palm of her hand. "Nothing so far, but I'm sure something will eventually turn up. The chickens and ducklings had to come from somewhere."

"Until then, the boys and I would be happy to take care of them for you. Wouldn't we, boys?"

When the triplets' expressions went from miserable to bright in a single beat, Clint's chest, already ballooning with emotion, expanded until he thought it might burst. And when the boys laughed, his heart nearly exploded.

He never would have seen himself, a confirmed bachelor, a cowboy too rugged to consider having a family of his own, championing a trio of youngsters— and more than that, enjoying it. He was startled to discover these boys meant something special to him.

Perhaps it was because he saw his younger self in them. They were without a father, after all. Maybe it was just a misplaced and, until this moment, entirely absent sense of chivalry, although he highly doubted it. A knight in shining armor he was not.

Whatever the reason, he cared about these kids—a lot. More than that, he cared about their pretty mama.

And he had no idea what to do with this new self-knowledge—except to champion them to the sheriff and save their chickens. That much he could do.

"I'll take personal responsibility for the feed," he added. "It won't cost the sheriff's department a penny."

"I can't let you do that," Olivia objected. "I'd love for the sheriff's department to allow the boys to keep the chickens and ducklings for the time being, but I'll take care of feeding costs myself."

Proud, stubborn woman. Clint admired her and was frustrated with her at the same time. As if she didn't have enough to worry about with her three boys and the struggling horse farm, she was now adding poultry to her growing list of concerns.

Clint had only himself to consider. He had money and nothing to spend it on. But he sensed arguing with her would only make her dig her heels in more. If he just showed up on her doorstep with a bag of chicken feed, she couldn't argue with him.

"Well, Sheriff?" he asked. "What do you think?"

"I think," she said, smiling broadly as relief flooded her features, "that the boys keeping the birds here is a wonderful idea. For now, at least."

She bent down to the boys' level, propping her hands on her knees. "What do you think, guys? Can you be my deputies and take care of this evidence for me? It's a really important job. Are you up for it?"

The triplets straightened and their gazes grew earnest, although their contagious smiles continued to linger.

Noah, the spokesman of the bunch, stepped forward. "Yes, ma'am. We'll take really good care of all of the chickens and ducklings. We promise."

"Okay, then," Lucy said with a solemn nod. "Please raise your right hands."

Noah and Levi raised their right hands. Caleb raised his left, then looked at his brothers, realized his error and quickly switched arms.

"Caleb is my southpaw," Olivia murmured to Clint with a chuckle. He joined in her laughter.

"I hereby pronounce the three of you, Caleb, Levi and Noah Kensington-Barlow, to be sheriff's deputies," Lucy proclaimed solemnly. "Do you promise to do your best to take care of the town's evidence?"

"Yes, ma'am," the three answered in unison.

"Then it's official. Hold on just a sec. I've got something for you in my vehicle."

Lucy left to retrieve whatever she'd been speaking of, and the boys' attention wandered back to the ducklings, leaving Clint and Olivia standing alone together.

All of a sudden the air grew thick and snapped with tension. Clint felt as if his brain had fled to another continent. He couldn't think of a single thing to say and doubted he could form words even if he had them.

And when his gaze met Olivia's, his internal distress became even more pronounced. He tried to swallow to relieve the scratchy lump in his throat but failed. His tongue felt like sandpaper.

She cast her soft smile at him, all rosy cheeks and glimmering blue eyes and full, pink-stained lips, and he was fairly certain his heart stopped beating. No air was clearing his burning lungs.

He jammed his hands into the front pockets of his jeans and rocked back on the heels of his boots. Something, anything, to relieve the hold she had on him.

He'd dated his fair share of women, but he'd never experienced anything like this in his life. Without a word, she tied him to her. It was crazy, but the only way he could describe it was that he felt as if whatever would make her smile would likewise make him happy.

"Here we go."

Clint hadn't even realized Lucy had returned. He

dropped his gaze and dug his toe into the dirt, hoping the sheriff hadn't seen him gaping at Olivia. Heat rushed to his face. It wasn't like him to get flustered over anything—especially a woman.

Lucy placed the boys in a line and with much ceremony stuck golden stickers in the shape of sheriff's badges on their chests.

"There, now. My three official deputies."

Olivia and Lucy applauded and Clint joined in, slowly coming out of his reverie.

Man, this woman was really doing a number on him. His tension mounted once again. What if this wasn't a one-time occurrence? What if he was going to get all tongue-tied every time he was around Olivia?

Oh, this wasn't good. Not good at all.

"Let me help you with the saddles," he said to Lucy. Anything to step away, have a moment to breathe. He certainly couldn't do that around Olivia.

Besides, he had a couple things he wanted to discuss with the sheriff that it would be better Olivia not know about, at least for now.

He didn't have time for small talk. Between him and Lucy, it wouldn't take much time to load up the saddles, so as soon as they were out of Olivia's earshot, Clint dived right into airing his concerns.

"When you find out who those birds belong to, can you please let me know first?"

Lucy glanced up at him, her gaze filled with a mixture of surprise and confusion. "Sure, I guess I can do that. But why would you want to know?"

"I'd like to make an offer to purchase the chickens and ducklings from their current owner. I can buy new birds if they'd like and will pay them twice the going rate. The boys have their hearts set on these particular chickens and I'd hate to disappoint them."

Lucy's eyes lit up with amusement and she smirked at him. "Oh-h-h," she said, stringing out the word. "I see."

He narrowed his gaze on her. "You see what?"

"This isn't about the triplets."

"Well, of course it's about the triplets. What else would it be about?"

He realized right after he asked the question that he shouldn't have—because he already knew the answer.

And so, apparently, did the sheriff.

"It wouldn't have anything to do with the boys' pretty mother, now would it?" she teased.

Clint groaned. He knew his face was flaming and the truth was blatantly obvious, so it wouldn't do him any good to deny it. He couldn't fool anyone, least of all the all-too-observant sheriff.

"Okay, yes. But can you keep this between the two of us? I'd like to surprise her and the boys with the news about the birds when the time is right."

"Of course." Lucy grinned. He supposed he was glad to give the sheriff something to smile about. She had her plate full with all that was going on with this Robin Hood nonsense. And speaking of the thieves...

"I think I may have found a connection in your case."

"Yeah?" The smile faded from her lips. Clint regretted that his words were the cause, but it couldn't be helped.

"I've been wondering why James and Libby's ranch hasn't been targeted by the thieves. They have a small spread but it's relatively prosperous, and other ranches their size have been robbed."

"And?"

"The picture you shared with Olivia and me the other day? Of that girl—Maddy? Something about it rang a bell with me but I didn't immediately know what it was."

"You know her?"

"No. I can't say that I do. But I did recognize the T-shirt she was wearing. The Future Ranchers logo? I remembered it because a couple of years ago I rescued a girl wearing that exact same T-shirt. She got lost in Deep Gulch on a day hike. I remember her because, unlike many lost and frightened hikers, she had the good sense to sit tight where she was instead of wandering around the mountains. Because she followed the wilderness safety tips she'd learned, it was only a couple of hours before Pav and I found her."

"I still don't understand. You say it wasn't Maddy. So what's the connection?"

He shook his head. "I'm not sure there is a link, except that like I said, they were wearing the same T-shirt. I thought maybe the two girls were friends. I checked my records. The young lady's name was Betsy McKay."

"McKay?"

"Yeah. She's Byron's niece, isn't she?" If Clint recalled correctly, Betsy's father had been the town drunk. Betsy eventually tired of living with him and fled town. "I don't know if it means anything. I just thought maybe since we think the Robin Hood guys are teenagers, they might have spared the Everharts' farm because I'd helped save a teenage girl they liked."

He shook his head. "I'm probably grasping at straws here. It could just as easily be that I'm not a member of the Cowboy League and the Everharts hardly ever participate. The thieves seem to be targeting league members. Or it might not have anything to do with me at all. Maybe they just haven't gotten to us yet."

"Maybe. I'll check into it, see if I can find a connection between Betsy and the thieves."

"At the Valentine Roundup, I was sizing up the McKay twins as possible suspects," Clint admitted, "but it's not like Gareth and Winston would rob their own father."

"No. You're probably right about that. Byron's ranch has been hit up twice, and the two branches of McKays were never that close to begin with. But there are some threads here. The thieves seem to appreciate the Future Ranchers program, or at least the girls who are participating in it right now. That is, I believe, why the Stillwaters have remained unscathed. Also, I'm fairly certain Maddy Coles and Betsy McKay were best friends at one point."

"It sounds like you're getting closer."

"Possibly. I think your information warrants you speaking to the Lone Star Cowboy League at their next official meeting. I'd like you to come to the chapter meeting a week from Tuesday night and share your thoughts with everyone."

Clint cringed inwardly. How had he managed to get talked into this? Privately sharing information with the sheriff was one thing. Public speaking was a whole other thing.

Getting up in front of a group of people and making a speech? He'd rather eat glass. "I don't know if I have anything useful, but I guess I can stop by and share what I know. If you're sure it will help."

"Stop by where?"

Clint hadn't seen Olivia approach and at the sound of her voice right next to his ear, a shiver of awareness went down his spine. She slipped her hand into the crook of his arm and his biceps tightened under her soft palm.

"I have some information regarding that photo Lucy showed us the other day."

"It's a slim lead," Lucy added, "but at this point we need every possible clue we can get."

"I'll go with you."

"You will?" Olivia's offer had come so far out of left field that he was completely unprepared to catch it.

"Absolutely." She squeezed his arm. "You've been my major channel of support since this whole incident with the thieves occurred. The least I can do is be there to show you some encouragement when you speak to the league."

"I—uh—" he stammered, and then cleared his throat and tried again. "Thank you."

"Oh, perfect." Lucy sent Clint a sly wink. "We'd be glad to have you, too, Olivia. You can share your thoughts about what happened here at your farm."

Perfect.

So Olivia was going to go with him and lend him support while he spoke to the Lone Star Cowboy

League. It was odd how comforting that felt to him, just to know she would be there by his side.

He remembered how eloquent she'd been at the Valentine Roundup. She had no problem speaking in a group, but he did. He wasn't keen on talking to people at all.

Except for Olivia. He couldn't seem to stop talking when she was around. Now, why was that?

Chapter Seven

Lone Star Cowboy League chapter president Carson Thorn brought the Tuesday evening meeting to order with a pound of his gavel. Small talk faded away as league members, including vice president Byron McKay, secretary Ingrid Edwards and treasurer Lynette Fields, along with other folks on the board, turned their attention to Carson.

Olivia was glad she could be here to support Clint, but she wished the sheriff hadn't added her to the docket. Surely Lucy would be a better candidate for sharing the Robin Hoods' latest movements. Olivia didn't feel she had much to offer.

Poor Clint. He was keeping his composure on the outside, but she knew he was quivering within. A public speaker he was not. Yes, he led trail rides, but that was out in his element, not captured here in a boardroom.

Clint glanced in her direction and she flashed him a reassuring smile, then reached for his hand under the table. His hands were a great deal larger than hers and the warmth of his palm penetrated the icy cold of her fingers.

She hoped her meaning was clear. They were in this together.

And that seemed only right. Clint had become a regular at Barlow Acres over the past week. They'd practically spent more time together than they had apart.

The first day he'd shown up with a bag of feed for the chickens and starter crumbles and leafy greens for the ducks. She probably should have been irritated that he'd ignored her wishes, but the truth was she hadn't had time to get to the feed store in town. The birds wouldn't have appreciated going without a meal because she was too busy to go get them food.

She'd figure out a way to pay Clint back. Eventually.

He'd spent the first afternoon out in the hutch playing with the ducklings with the triplets. When she'd gone to check on them, she'd discovered that they'd rigged together a working waterwheel to go along with the waterfall and slide.

"How clever," she'd exclaimed, crouching to watch the ducklings frolicking in their small pond.

"It was Mr. Clint's idea," Levi had told her.

"But the muggles made it," he'd countered. "I didn't have to help them one bit. You've got bright sons, Mama."

She'd preened. And she'd invited him to share dinner with them. It was the least she could do. Which had led to bedtime stories for the boys and then a long, cozy talk between Olivia and Clint that lasted well into the evening.

He'd shown up every evening since and had spent the entire last weekend with them. At first he'd had one excuse or another for why he'd come, but eventually he hadn't offered or needed an explanation at all.

He'd even attended church with her and the boys on Sunday morning, freshly shaved and in black dress pants and a starched white button-down shirt that was clearly just out of its packaging. He cleaned up well, but Olivia found she actually preferred him with a couple days' growth of beard on his face and in well-worn jeans and a denim shirt.

Gossip flew when she and Clint had attended church together, but she didn't care. Something special was growing between them. She was experiencing the giddy feelings of attraction to Clint that she hadn't believed, as a single mother with three young, precocious boys, she would ever be blessed to experience again.

Clint was special. He spent as much time with the triplets as he did her, and he gave them his full attention whenever he was with them. With her he was comfortable, and that was saying a lot.

There were no dates between them, no flirty texts or silly phone calls.

He just showed up at the farm and had become an integral part of their family in just over a week. She was already starting to depend on him in more ways than she had ever believed possible. And she thought he might be feeling the same way about her.

Like now. His hand was in hers in a very public venue. Granted, their fingers were laced together under the table, where no one could see them, but she had little doubt it would matter to Clint who noticed they were together, nor what they thought about it.

Whatever else Clint was, he was his own man.

And she was glad to be by his side. Hopefully, public speaking wouldn't seem as daunting to him when she was near to provide support. If he got nervous he could just look at her.

"Sheriff Benson," Carson said after the board had approved the minutes from the last meeting, "would you please bring the board up-to-date on where we stand in the Robin Hood investigation?"

"Yes," Byron agreed. "Please tell us that you are finally doing your job."

Clint's grasp on Olivia's hand tightened. She could feel his muscles coil with tension and, frankly, she shared his agitation. Byron McKay simply didn't know when to keep his mouth shut.

"Byron," Carson warned. "You're out of order. The sheriff has the floor."

"By all means," Byron sneered, gesturing for Lucy to continue.

"It still appears the thieves are specifically targeting league members in their robberies. They don't appear as particular when it comes to gifting others with what they've stolen. Some folks are league members, others are not, and of course, many gift recipients are teenagers and even children. Olivia, would you please report on what happened at your farm a week ago Saturday?"

"Certainly." She stood to address the board. Clint winked at her.

"A week ago Saturday, the Robin Hoods visited my farm while the boys and I were out for the day. They left my sons new children's saddles, three chickens, half a dozen ducklings and a note."

She frowned. "It was a very thoughtful gift, and the note indicated it was specifically targeted to my boys. Whoever these thieves are, they knew my sons were riding with well-used adult-sized saddles. And the triplets had been talking about wanting to raise chickens and ducks of their own. The thieves must have overheard them somewhere, which means they are part of our community. They blend in because they are one of us. They're local young men who don't stand out in a crowd."

"Thank you, Olivia," Carson said. "You've been very helpful in assisting us in narrowing our Robin Hoods' profiles."

Olivia sat down and exhaled. She enjoyed speaking to groups and the adrenaline that went along with it, and she embraced the snap of electricity along her nerves. Clint caught her gaze and silently mouthed, *"Well done."*

Her stomach fluttered. His opinion held extra weight with her.

Clint was up next. He was better at hiding his fear of public speaking than she would have been if she'd been in his shoes. He surprised her. He was a mountain man and a loner and was by nature an introvert, but he spoke clearly and powerfully, informing the league members of his theory on why the Everharts' ranch hadn't been visited by the thieves when all the others in the area had been. He spoke of his possible connection with Betsy McKay, who had been a member of the league-run Future Ranchers, because he'd rescued her when she'd gotten lost hiking.

Lucy continued where Clint left off. She'd investigated the issue, trying to solidify the link, but at best it was tenuous. The thieves appeared to have a special liking for the Future Ranchers program, or at least the girls who were part of it. Maddy Coles, the recipient of special attention by the Robin Hoods and likely someone at least one of the thieves was sweet on, had been best friends with Betsy before she fled town. Maddy didn't know where Betsy now resided, so Lucy couldn't follow up with the girl herself.

"It doesn't necessarily follow that Betsy knows our thieves," the sheriff reminded the board. "Although at this point it seems likely. Just as we suspect one of them knows and possibly even cares for Maddy, it's possible the thieves haven't hit Clint's foster parents' ranch because of what he did for Betsy."

"I can't imagine why," Byron said, leaning back in his chair and threading his fingers over his ample belly. "Why are we even talking about this? Betsy is long gone and no one knows where she is right now."

"We need all the leads we can get," Lucy reminded him. "So far we've come up empty-handed."

Carson inserted his leadership before Byron could snap back. "Is there anything else we need to know?"

The sheriff was a strong, capable woman, but Olivia was positive she saw her face pale.

"Actually, there is one more thing." Lucy scowled and dragged in a deep breath.

Olivia slid her hand back into Clint's and gripped it tightly, sensing she wasn't going to like whatever Lucy said next.

"As some of you already know, the thefts abruptly

stopped after I confiscated the saddles from the Barlows' farm and the baler from the Donners' ranch."

That wasn't exactly a bad thing in Olivia's estimation. No news was good news, right? Maybe the teenagers had tired of their pranks or had finally wised up to the fact that they might get caught.

"It's not that I'm in a hurry for them to attempt more thefts," Lucy clarified, "but I think that's the only way we're going to catch them. They've been getting braver, and with that, less cautious. It's only a matter of time before they slip up, and when they do, I'm going to be there to catch them."

"But now you say they've stopped their activity," Grady Stillwater reiterated. A recently returned special ops veteran, he stretched in his seat to accommodate his injured leg. "Any idea why that might be?"

"My guess would be that we're frustrating them," Olivia offered. "What good does it do for them to steal things and try to give them to those they consider less fortunate if the sheriff turns right around and confiscates the goods? We're thwarting them here."

"Good point," Carson agreed. "They do seem to be primarily motivated by their misguided notion of robbing from the rich to give to the poor."

"Misguided?" Byron roared. "These thieves are the lowest of the low, takin' a man's hard-won stock and equipment and giving it to the undeserving. They'd better have the book thrown at them when you catch them, and it better happen soon. I demand a full accounting for all the crimes they've committed."

Clint's muscles tensed at Byron's words about

those the thieves had chosen to gift with their plun-
der. Olivia was afraid he was going to spring from
his seat and throttle the man. She knew exactly why,
too, and it warmed her heart. Byron had insulted her,
at least in a roundabout way, and Clint had her back.

Olivia pulled his hand onto her lap and squeezed
hard, trying to communicate to him without words
that Byron's blustering wasn't worth Clint's efforts.
The insults didn't have any effect on her, but Clint's
defensive reaction made her want to sing.

"It's true the thefts appear to have stopped," Lucy
agreed, ignoring Byron entirely. "However, their actions have not." She paused. "Last night I had a rock
thrown through my kitchen window."

Olivia gasped. Silence filled the room for a split
second and then everyone burst into chatter at once.

Carson pounded his gavel, but people were talking over each other and the noise level was too high
for him to be heard. Clint stood, put his thumb and
forefinger to his lips and whistled shrilly.

It was enough to make everyone pause and look
in his direction. He held up his hands. "Please, take
your seats. We aren't going to get anywhere if everyone is speaking at once."

Even if he didn't particularly care to be in the lime-
light, Clint was a natural leader, and it didn't take long
for the league members to settle down.

"Were you hurt?" Carson asked Lucy, who'd remained standing, hugging herself with her arms in
an instinctually defensive posture.

"No. They weren't aiming at me. They were sending us a message. There was a note wrapped around

the rock with a rubber band." She ran her gaze across the crowded room. "There were only two words typed on the paper—*Not fair.*"

"What's not fair?" Byron growled. "I'll tell you what's not fair. Not *fair* is having your ranch robbed, not once, but twice. Not *fair* is having your cattle lifted right from under you. *That's* what's not fair."

"You've made yourself perfectly clear, Byron," Carson said with an edge of impatience to his voice.

Clint had gone well beyond impatient with Byron McKay. That man had flat out insulted Olivia in front of a room of people, implying that she was lazy and didn't work hard.

As if Byron had ever worked a day in his life. Everything he owned had been handed to him on a silver platter.

Olivia worked harder than anyone Clint knew. She spent her days out with her horses and took care of her three precocious—and precious—boys at night and on weekends. And she did it all by herself. No ranch hands. No nannies. Frankly, Clint didn't know how she did it, but one thing was for certain. Byron shouldn't be cutting her down.

"I think that strengthens the profile of our thieves," Carson said.

Lucy nodded. "I agree. Another note with juvenile wording, just like at the Valentine Roundup."

"So we're looking for two or more teenage or young adult males," Carson said, ticking his list off with his fingers. "They're able-bodied and strong enough to lift heavy equipment and manipulate large-ticket items. They know ranching, as demonstrated by their gift of a baler to the Donners. And they're local, since they knew about the Barlow boys' desire to raise chickens. Last, they are probably involved with some of the local girls—Maddy Coles for sure and possibly Betsy McKay, as well."

"And they are holding a grudge against the members of the Lone Star Cowboy League," Olivia reminded them.

"Right." Carson knocked his closed fist against the tabletop. "We need to make a more concerted effort to narrow our search to league members with teenage or young adult sons or grandsons."

"Present company excepted, of course," Byron insisted. "You don't have to bother with my boys."

Clint was about to protest, but he saw Carson catch Lucy's gaze and understood they were going to go ahead with their plans and ignore Byron's presumptuous rant.

Hopefully with the new profile, the sheriff would finally be able to catch the thieves, so the folks in Little Horn could rest easy and go on with their lives without the constant fear of being robbed.

But where did that leave Clint?

His throat tightened, clouding with emotion. Once the thieves were behind bars, there would be no reason for him to visit Olivia and the boys anymore. He'd told himself that his daily visits to Barlow Acres were for their protection, to check up on them and ensure their safety. But that was no longer true, and maybe it never had been.

He was personally attracted to Olivia and he went to Barlow Acres because he wanted to be around her.

Her boys were a welcome part of the package. With Levi, Caleb and Noah, he got to do all those things he'd always hoped his father would have done with him when he was a young boy. When he was with Olivia and the triplets, he felt as if he was making up for lost time in his life.

And whenever Olivia slipped her hand into his, or touched his arm, or smiled up at him, he felt like a million bucks, like the most blessed man on earth. It was no accident that he'd returned to church just as his relationship with Olivia had started to bloom.

Relationship.

It was a heavy word, and one that in any other situation would have sent him literally running for the safety and anonymity of his beloved mountains.

Not this time.

This time, he wanted to stay.

It was Olivia who should be running, as far and as fast as she could go. He was no good for her. He was so screwed up inside that no one could fix him. He didn't even know what a long-term relationship ought to look like. And as wonderful as he felt whenever he interacted with the triplets, he could hardly be the father figure they needed in their lives.

He scoffed inwardly. What did he know about being a father? His own father had cared so little for him that he'd abandoned him. Trying to pursue a long-term relationship was simply setting himself up for failure, and with that, Olivia and the triplets would also crash and burn.

What had Clint been thinking, spending all this time with Olivia? Giving her the wrong impression?

He hadn't been thinking at all. He'd been acting on his emotions.

He should end this relationship now—*before* it got too serious. It didn't matter that it was already serious to him. He wasn't who counted here.

His chest tightened when he thought about the consequences of his actions. The triplets would be disappointed when he stopped dropping by the farm, but they were young. They'd get over it. It might take Olivia a little longer, but she'd find another man, one who could offer her and the boys the life Clint could not.

That it completely gutted him to even imagine Olivia with another man was beside the point. This was about what was best for her and her family.

Resolved to quietly remove himself from her life, he waited as Carson wrapped up the league meeting. There was little to discuss besides the recent thefts. A few housekeeping issues and they were dismissed.

"You seem distant," Olivia remarked as they walked back to his truck, still hand in hand, their fingers tightly linked. "What are you thinking about?"

He couldn't even meet her gaze, much less speak. He swallowed the lump of emotion in his throat and shrugged noncommittally.

"I know," she said, as if he'd just offered her a full explanation.

"You do?" His pulse hammered.

"I feel the same way."

"You *do*?" He knew he was repeating himself, but she had just floored him with her statement. Here he was trying to figure out a way to let her down easily and she was doing the deed for him.

He should be relieved. So why did it feel as if his heart had just been ripped from his chest?

"You don't believe we're completely out of the woods yet, do you?"

"What?" He scrambled to fill in the blanks but felt as if she'd yanked him down a different, unfamiliar path and he was struggling just to catch up.

"The thieves aren't finished, are they? They may have stopped briefly for now, for whatever reason, but it's not over, is it? Lucy getting a rock thrown through her window? That's terrifying."

Olivia sounded concerned, maybe even frightened. And she was right. The Robin Hoods were still out there somewhere and they still posed a viable threat. Rocks through windows? They were stepping up their game.

And Clint was thinking about exiting Olivia's life right now? What kind of man would think about leaving a woman when she needed him most?

They rode in silence for a few minutes until he pulled his truck into her long gravel driveway and cut the engine. The whole drive home he'd been trying to work out what he should say. It was complicated. He wanted to reassure her without giving her a false sense of hope regarding their relationship—but how?

A neighbor girl was watching the triplets and he knew Olivia was anxious to relieve her. He walked her to the door, waited until she had the key in the lock and then turned back toward his truck.

He had nothing. Hopefully after a good night's sleep he'd know what he should do, what he should say.

"Clint?"

He froze but did not turn.

"Would you like to come in for a while? The boys are already sleeping but…" She paused. "It's been kind of a rough night. I could use some company right now."

Joy warmed his chest. He shouldn't want this. It would only make things that much worse for both of them when it was time for him to walk away.

But tonight she needed reassurance. She needed safety. She needed him near her.

He whirled on the toes of his boots and stretched out his hand to her.

Tomorrow would be soon enough for goodbyes.

Chapter Eight

Olivia couldn't quite put her finger on it, but something was off with Clint tonight. He'd been his usual charming and goofy self when he'd picked her up earlier in the evening, but as time went on he'd become more and more reserved and distant until he was barely speaking to her at all.

His withdrawal sent a skitter of alarm through her, but she did her best to ignore it. If he needed a friend, she wanted to be there for him, just as he'd proved he'd be there for her.

Something was bothering him, and she wasn't convinced it had anything to do with the recent thefts. No—it was something else, something more personal, and she wasn't about to let him go home to an empty house until he felt better. A cup of hot tea with honey wouldn't solve all his problems, but it was a good place to start.

That, and a listening ear and an understanding heart. She could give him those things.

She propped herself on one side of the sofa and tucked her legs beneath her, expecting Clint to sit down next to her, maybe even hold her hand, as he had their last few evenings together. Instead, he slumped into the armchair across from her and folded his arms over his chest in a closed posture.

"Okay, spill." She lifted an eyebrow at him. "Something's bothering you. Out with it."

He frowned and grunted noncommittally. He certainly wasn't making this easy on either one of them. She hoped he realized he didn't have to play the tough guy for her benefit. She didn't expect him to be a superhero all the time.

"You're worried about James and Libby," she guessed. "You think you might be wrong about your theory regarding Betsy McKay and believe the thieves might hit the Everharts' ranch, after all."

That was odd. She was almost positive it was *relief* that she noticed briefly flashing through his eyes, but he wasted no time before grasping on to her words.

"Well, sure, I worry about them. They're vulnerable out there. Their ranch is farther from town than most of the others, and neither one of them is in the best of health. If the thieves are getting more brazen, and it seems like they are, what if they try to rob the ranch in broad daylight and James or Libby happens upon them?"

Clint sighed deeply and his gaze dropped to his fisted hands. "The young men haven't been violent so far, thankfully, but there's no telling what they'd do if they feel like they are threatened or backed into a corner."

"Oh, Clint." Olivia crossed the distance between them and sat on the corner of the armchair, covering his clenched fists with her hands. "Surely the thieves aren't dangerous. They're probably just a couple of misguided teenagers whose silly pranks got out of hand."

"Probably," he agreed, but he didn't sound as if he meant it. The Robin Hoods, whoever they were, had left "silly" behind them a long time ago, with the theft of the street sign. They were major cattle rustlers now.

"Libby and James employ a couple of ranch hands, don't they?"

"Yes, but the wranglers don't work every day. And at night they go home to their families. Besides, what good will it do if they are out herding cattle and the thieves are busy robbing the house? I'd feel much better if James and Libby had someone with them all the time until the Robin Hoods are behind bars."

"You mean *you* wish *you* could be with them." Olivia knew exactly how he was feeling, and she empathized completely. "And so you should be."

"Yeah, I suppose I do want to be there for them. But I can't be everywhere all the time. I'm gone most days and often lead overnight guide trips. I'm hardly at the ranch at all anymore."

She stood abruptly, her heart hammering. She had no right to expect him to be here with her and the boys when his foster mom and dad needed him. She was taking up what little time he could give to the Everharts.

"You should go," she whispered, her voice cracking with emotion.

He stood, confusion masking his features for a moment before his expression hardened.

"Yeah, I guess I should get going." His voice was low and scratchy.

She walked him to the door and then followed him out onto the porch, not quite ready for him to go. Something still felt off between them, and she didn't want to leave it that way. She searched for the right words—for *any* words that would let him know how much she cared about him. That he wasn't alone.

That she was there for him.

Nothing came. Not a single word. He stepped off the porch and reached for the door of his truck.

"Clint, wait." She dashed forward and caught his elbow. He turned to face her, so close that she could hear the sharp rasp of his breath. So close she breathed in the warm musk of his aftershave. When he captured her gaze, her own breath caught in her throat. With only the moon and stars for illumination, his eyes gleamed a burnished gold.

"Yeah? What is it?" He bent his head but never took his eyes off hers.

"I—I—" Oh, why wouldn't the words come?

She tried again. "I want you to go be with James and Libby. I do. They need you right now. But—" Her breath escaped her and she couldn't finish the sentence.

"But?" he prompted, chuckling softly, sounding just a little bit more like the man she'd come to care for.

I'll be here.

The boys and I need you.

Nothing sounded the way she wanted it to, and even if it had, the words eluded her.

Her gaze dropped to his lips. One side of his mouth was curled into that crooked grin that unearthed a swarm of butterflies in her stomach. The one that sent her heart drumming out an erratic tattoo.

"Olivia?"

She had nothing. Nothing except…

She didn't think. She only followed where her heart was leading her, and had been leading her since the night of the Valentine Roundup when Miss Betty Leland had pressed a pink paper heart into her hand.

Olivia Barlow

Clint Daniels

She reached for his face, reveling in the scrape of his whiskered jaw under her palms. She slid one hand into the thick hair at the back of his neck and drew him down to her.

"Olivia, I—" he groaned, but she didn't let him complete his thought. She closed her eyes and pressed her lips to his.

He stiffened for a moment and her heart skipped a beat as she realized she might just have made the biggest mistake of her life. She'd crossed an unspoken barrier between them.

Before she even had time to work up a good blush, Clint wrapped his arms around her waist, drawing her closer to him. She had initiated the kiss, but he promptly took the lead, tenderly brushing his lips over hers again and again, murmuring her name between each kiss.

He did care.

His hands came up to frame her face and she

dropped hers to rest against his muscular chest. She could feel the rapid thumping of his heart under her palm.

He leaned his forehead against hers and stared into her eyes, his breath mingling with hers.

Her heart was elated and she felt as light as a feather. A good breeze could have blown her away. She wasn't entirely certain her feet were touching the ground at all.

It was Clint who anchored her, with his gaze and with his gentle touch.

And this was just the beginning.

A groan emerged from deep in Clint's chest. He dropped his hands and stepped away from her so fast she nearly fell over. The air around her turned cold. Empty. She ached to be back in the warmth of his arms again, but he had already turned away and was opening the cab door of his truck.

"Clint?"

What had just happened? Where was he going?

He tossed his hat on the seat and shoved his fingers through his hair.

"That should not have happened."

His cold words pelted her like a sleet storm, her emotions fading into darkness as the sun exited her life. Shivering, she wrapped her arms around herself and clutched her shoulders.

Surely she'd misunderstood.

Clint ran a hand down his face and sighed deeply.

"This was a mistake. You need to turn around and walk back into your house and forget about this. About me."

Anger filled her. He'd just crumpled up her heart and tossed it in the trash can as if it was yesterday's news. How dare he downplay her emotions and the moment they had just shared? He did not get to tell her how to feel.

"Can you do that?" she challenged. "Just get in your truck and drive away and *forget about* our time together?"

His brows lowered over his stormy eyes and he frowned, but he didn't deny his feelings. She pressed her advantage.

"Tell me this meant nothing to you," she challenged, her anger unfurling.

He jerked his head from side to side. "You know I can't do that."

She folded her arms and stared him down. A wild mix of emotions churned through her. She was absolutely furious with Clint right now, and hurt, too. But most of all, she cared about him.

Despite everything that had just happened, she cared about him.

A lot.

"I'm not good for you," he ground out, his voice husky.

She laughed, but it was dry and without mirth. "Don't you think I should be the judge of that?"

"I kissed you when I can't make a commitment to you—or the boys."

"If I remember correctly, I was the one who kissed you. And I wasn't asking you to put a ring on my finger."

He winced. "I'm not the kind of man who would toy with a single mom and her three children."

"Is that what you're doing? Toying with me?" She knew she was baiting him, but couldn't seem to stop herself. Her dignity was in shreds, and she wanted him to hurt the way he was hurting her.

No. That was wrong. She dragged in a deep breath and took a mental step backward. No matter how she felt, tit for tat wasn't what she'd been brought up to believe. Jesus would have her turn the other cheek.

"I'm sorry. I shouldn't have said that. I know you're not toying with me."

"No," he agreed, his voice an octave lower than usual. "I'm not. And that's why I'm getting into my truck right now and driving away."

This time she didn't stop him. She clenched her jaw so tight that her teeth hurt, but she did not stop him.

Instead, she stood silently as he drove away, her heart shattering into millions of sharp, painful shards.

She was alone. Again.

She didn't know what she was going to tell the triplets about why Clint had stopped coming around. She didn't know how she was going to get through the days to come. How she was going to keep living, keep breathing, or even how her heart would keep beating.

Clint was gone. And he wasn't coming back.

Clint was thankful that his business was slow in the early spring. He spent the next few days nursing his internal wounds by doing what he'd always done when he needed space. He'd taken Pav and gone camping in the Deep Gulch Mountains, spending his days searching for a hidden treasure he was fairly certain did not exist and spending his nights sleeping under the stars—stars that twinkled the way they'd shone on the night he and Olivia had kissed.

Everything reminded him of Olivia, and every time he thought of her, the pain started all over again.

When he was ten years old, he'd gotten into a fight with an older boy at the state home he was living in at the time. The boy had provoked him, but it hadn't taken much to light a fire under Clint. Even that young, he'd been a scrapper and could have taken on the older and larger boy, but the kid had friends who'd ganged up on Clint, beating him to the ground and kicking him repeatedly. He'd come away from that encounter with three cracked ribs and more bruises than he could count. But that was nothing compared to the ache in his chest that he was currently experiencing.

Not even the peace and serenity of Deep Gulch, nor the intense majesty of God's creation could touch Clint's soul right now.

The only way to fix what was ailing him would be to return to Olivia and beg her forgiveness. And that he could not—would not—do. Not because of some misguided sense of pride or male ego. He'd gladly humble himself if it meant he would have the blessing of becoming a part of Olivia's and the triplets' lives once again.

No, this had nothing to do with him at all.

It was all about what was best for Olivia and her boys, and he was not what was best for them. Sure, it seemed as if he meshed into her family perfectly—building the hutch, listening to bedtime prayers and tucking the boys in at night were now some of his most precious memories. Even more valued was the time he'd spent with Olivia, sharing their innermost thoughts and dreams with each other.

He'd never felt as close to another person in his life

as he had during those evening talks with Olivia. It was as if she was an extension of his own being. And without her, he felt as if part of his body had been carved out of him.

His heart.

Because as much as might have been going well between them now, as perfect and amazing as the kiss they'd shared had been, it was only a matter of time before he would mess things up. The niggling fear of abandonment he'd struggled with since the day his father had left him rose within him, filling his chest with anxiety.

What did he know about relationships, never mind being a good father figure for the boys? They deserved better than he could offer them.

He didn't trust himself, so how could he ask Olivia to trust him with her heart?

He picked his way off one of the marked trails on foot, having chosen not to bring his gelding on this trip. As always, he kept an eye out for signs of the treasure.

Suddenly the sound of sirens rent the air. Several vehicles' worth of sirens.

Pav heard them, too. The golden retriever had been out gallivanting in the deeply wooded area but quickly returned to Clint's side, quivering with excitement. For Pav, sirens meant it was go time.

For Clint, too, for that matter. It probably wasn't a search and rescue incident or he would already have been called in, but someone might be hurt or in danger, and besides, he was curious. It might just be the sheriff pulling over a speeder, but he decided it was worth checking out. It wasn't as if he had anything else important to do.

He changed direction and headed toward the sound of the sirens. He'd been hiking well into the mountains, and on foot, even at a brisk pace, it took him a good forty-five minutes to reach the trailhead at Pine Meadow, where the sirens were coming from.

His stomach tumbled when he got there. This was where he'd spent his first full day with Olivia and the triplets and his memories momentarily overwhelmed him.

How long would it be before everything stopped reminding him of Olivia?

He'd half expected the police or ambulance or whatever it had been to be long gone by now, but as he broke into the clearing, he was surprised to find not only two of the sheriff's vehicles, but two fire trucks and an ambulance.

Something major was going down.

His nerves were on fire as he jogged down the mountainside to join the group huddled near the ambulance. Lucy was among them, her familiar notebook open in her hand and her expression grim.

"Did someone get hurt?" Clint asked, his lungs burning from exertion as he tried to catch his breath. He propped his hands on his knees and gasped for air.

"Not hurt," A. J. Salomen, Little Horn's fire chief, said regretfully. "Some local rock climbers left the trail to explore Cathedral Ridge."

"Those rocks are off-limits. It's clearly marked here at the trailhead." Clint gestured to the warning sign that cautioned hikers against climbing hazardous Cathedral Ridge, which was full of loose rocks and gravel.

"Apparently, they ignored the warning. And so did someone else. The rock climbers came upon a body at the base of the cliff, hidden behind overgrown bushes."

That was a shame. Too often people didn't use common sense when it came to mountain excursions. They'd just get it in their heads that they wanted to climb some rock or other and off they'd go, giving no thought whatsoever to their safety or the laws of the land. Never mind if experts had warned against it or if it was illegal to do so.

And this was what resulted when they did.

"Have you identified the body?" he asked grimly, bracing himself for the possibility of it being a name he knew. He hadn't heard of any missing persons in Little Horn, but he wasn't exactly in the loop where gossip was concerned.

"This accident wasn't recent," Lucy informed him. "The body has been there for quite some time, possibly years. We've determined that he's a male, but we know little more than that. We're going to have to wait for the forensic pathology report to know for sure when and how he died, but it's reasonable to believe he was climbing the rocks and slipped and fell to his death.

Like Luke.

Clint's gut clenched. The news of hikers finding a dead body in the Deep Gulch Mountains would quickly spread throughout Little Horn. When Olivia heard of it, he imagined it would send her into an emotional tailspin as she recalled all the pain and despair she'd experienced when her husband passed away from his accident.

Clint knew how difficult the time had been for her. She'd shared with him the emotions she'd experienced during that dark time of her life. This news would gut her.

Who would be there to hold Olivia tight, to comfort her through her grief and get her to the other side?

"No identification?" he asked, ignoring the emotions roiling through him. "Wallet? Driver's license? Credit cards?"

He already knew the answer to that question and wasn't sure why he'd asked. Obviously, the first thing the sheriff would do would be to check for identification.

"He wasn't carrying a wallet, and what's left of his clothing is nondescript," Lucy said. "The only item of note that we discovered on him was this."

She held up what looked like a tarnished silver pocket watch with the shape of a cross etched into the metal, barely visible due to time and the elements.

All the air left Clint's lungs in a rush and it was all he could do not to double over in pain.

It wasn't a pocket watch. It was a compass.

And it belonged to his father.

He didn't even need to open it to be sure, although he knew his dad's initials were engraved within. His father had promised to pass that compass on to him one day.

Clint squeezed his eyes closed as a thunderstorm of emotions overwhelmed him, tossing him to and fro like a sapling in a tornado.

His father was dead.

Dead.

As bad as it was to have thought his dad had abandoned him, Clint had always assumed his father was out there somewhere, living a narcissistic life without a single thought for his son, but living nonetheless.

Dad was dead.

His thoughts swirled around in his head and he forgot to breathe, quickly becoming so light-headed that he had to look for a place to sit before he fell down.

The back doors of the ambulance were open and he stumbled toward it, slumping onto the bumper just as his legs gave out.

He scrubbed a hand down his face and tried to inhale, struggling for self-control. The last thing he wanted to do was lose it in front of other people. He wished he was alone.

He wished he was with Olivia.

Olivia.

The one person he trusted to hold him while he grieved. She was the only one who would understand exactly how he felt, and he couldn't imagine anyone else in the world who could make him feel better.

"Clint?" Lucy put a steadying hand on his shoulder. "Are you all right?"

He shook his head, struggling to find his voice.

"I know," he started, but his throat closed abruptly. He forced himself to breathe through it. "I know who the man is."

"You do? Who is it?" Lucy asked gently.

"My father." He pressed his fists into his thighs and fought for control. "I recognize the compass. If you open it up, you'll find his initials engraved inside.

"*O.T.D.* Owen Thaddeus Daniels."

A.J. blew out a low whistle. "Wow. I'm sorry, buddy. That's tough news."

"And a horrible way to find out about it. I'm so sorry for your loss," Lucy added. "This must be terribly painful for you to bear. If there's anything I can do…" She let her sentence dangle.

He shook his head. Nothing—*nothing*—could possibly ever make this right.

"Would you like me to call Olivia?" she asked, her voice lined with compassion.

His heart jolted to life at the sound of Olivia's name. He jerked his head up, meeting Lucy's kind gaze.

Every single part of him begged him to say yes. He'd never needed or wanted anything as much as he needed Olivia right now. He clenched his jaw until the wave of panic passed.

"No." He ground out the word from between dry lips. "Please don't bother Olivia." Now was not the time to try to explain that he'd ended his relationship with Olivia almost before it began.

Lucy's eyebrows disappeared under her hairline. Her confusion was understandable.

"I could use a ride back to my truck," he said, trying to focus the conversation, and his thoughts, elsewhere. "I'm parked at the Evergreen Heights trailhead. And—" He swallowed hard. "—I'd like to see the body, if that's okay."

Lucy squeezed his shoulder. "It's severely decomposed," she reminded him. "And we have to send the body to forensics to determine the cause of death. But afterward we'll release it to you. I promise."

He gritted his teeth and nodded. He'd found his father, and now he had to bury him.

"I'm going to need to ask you a few questions when you're ready to talk about it," Lucy said.

He was never going to be ready to talk about it. His entire world view had just come crashing down around him. Everything he believed about love and family and commitment was wrong. His new and tenuous relationship with God was being tested through fire.

How could the Lord have let this happen?

So many years.

"Let's talk about it now," he insisted.

"Clint, are you sure? You're not looking so hot right now. Maybe you should take some time to process all this before I interview you."

"I'm not feeling so hot right now, but waiting isn't going to make it any easier."

Lucy sighed and nodded. "Okay, if you're sure."

"I am."

"And you don't want me to call Olivia? I'm sure she'd come down here to support you."

"No." He wished Lucy would stop pushing the subject, because if she didn't, he was likely to break down and make that phone call. She was right about Olivia. No matter what had gone down between them, she would be here for him in an instant if he asked. And then when this was all over he would have to break her heart—and his—all over again.

"All right. When was the last time you saw your dad?"

"If I don't miss my guess, the last time I saw him was the day he died."

"Go on."

"It was my sixth birthday, so that would be twenty-six years ago. He took me up to Deep Gulch for a treasure hunt. He'd hidden my birthday present in a lockbox somewhere in the mountains, or at least I think he was going to. He told me to stay put where I was and that he'd be back soon to get me and then we'd go find it."

Clint's eyes stung and he pinched the bridge of his nose with his thumb and forefinger. "I waited and waited but…" His breath turned ragged "He didn't come back. Ever."

"So let me reiterate what you've said to make sure I've got this right. Your father just left a six-year-old in the woods by himself?"

"He'd been taking me to this spot in the mountains since I was old enough to walk. It was a familiar clearing. I don't think he meant to be gone more than fifteen minutes or so."

Lucy scowled. "That's far too long to leave a six-year-old boy alone."

Clint shrugged wearily. "Does it matter?"

"No, I suppose not. So he left you in this clearing to go hide your gift, and then he somehow fell off Cathedral Ridge and died."

Clint shook his head. "That's what I don't get. Why would he have been on Cathedral Ridge? Even back then it was forbidden due to safety issues. My dad was a mountain man. Why would he have done something so foolish as to climb a ridge he knew was risky?"

"I don't know. We may never know."

"And you didn't find my gift? It wasn't on him?"

"Well, it's hard to say, given that we don't know

what it was, nor whether it would have survived the elements. But to answer your question, no. We searched the area quite thoroughly. The only thing we found was the compass."

"Can I have it?" He had no mementos of his father's. He'd wanted to forget the man had ever existed. But now...

"As soon as we've wrapped up this case I'll make sure it gets to you," Lucy promised. "It shouldn't take long."

"You know what's the craziest part of all? I kept looking for that treasure."

"Yeah? But you never found it?"

"No. Like you said, it's probably long gone by now." But he'd never searched at the base of Cathedral Ridge. Why would he look somewhere both he and his father had known was off-limits? He'd been certain his father would never go there.

Not that it mattered now. The sheriff's department had combed the area and had found nothing.

He'd been looking for the treasure to bring him closure. And there was no more substantial closure than death.

The death of his father. The death of his budding relationship with Olivia. How much more could a man bear?

Chapter Nine

Shoe shopping.

Olivia had been told it was the prescription for every illness, even sicknesses of the heart.

Oh, who was she kidding? Certainly not herself. There was no cure for what ailed her, no relief for the peculiar combination of ache and emptiness that had invaded her chest where her heart used to be. But if she didn't get out of the house, she was going to drive herself crazy overthinking every little thing.

Even taking care of her herd didn't help her. Usually she felt an inexplicable peace among her quarter horses, but no matter how hard she tried to forget, she couldn't seem to shake off her glumness. Rejection didn't come easy.

Shoe shopping in Austin wasn't the answer, but at least it would get her out of Little Horn for the afternoon. A friend whose son was on the same T-ball team as the triplets had offered to pick them up after school and take them to practice, giving Olivia some much-needed free time.

Her mind wandered as she drove through the small

town's main corridor, heading for the highway leading to Austin. It was an easy drive with little traffic, and she'd taken it dozens of times over the years. The most important factor drivers around Little Horn needed to be aware of while navigating country roads was the possibility of loose livestock wandering into the way, or any of a wide assortment of Texas wildlife bounding onto the road in front of a car.

As she reached the narrow bridge across the shallow river that bordered the south end of town, she slowed her speed. A sedan was barreling down the road toward her, moving somewhat erratically and way too fast for a county road. The driver, an unfamiliar young blonde-haired woman, was apparently oblivious to the fact that the bridge was too narrow for two vehicles, so Olivia braked and pulled to the side to allow the other car to cross first. She hoped the stranger would at least slow her speed as she entered Little Horn town limits.

Olivia lifted her hand to wave at the young woman just as a jackrabbit darted onto the bridge in front of the sedan.

Olivia's heart leaped into her throat and every organ and muscle buzzed as she watched the scene unfold as if in slow motion.

The woman's expression was etched in terror as she stomped on her brakes and yanked her wheel to the right to avoid hitting the rabbit.

Belatedly realizing her car had nowhere to go, she jerked the sedan to the left, but overcompensated and turned too far.

Wheels squealed against the pavement. Gravel

flew. The sedan broke through the barrier and went airborne, seemingly suspended out of time.

And then it dropped like a brick, the front of the car crumpling against the riverbank while the back tires sank into the mud at the water's edge.

The jackrabbit dashed away without a scratch.

"Oh, Lord," Olivia prayed aloud. "Oh, Lord. Please let her be okay."

She fished her cell phone out of her purse.

Please, God. Please, God. Please, God.

She'd never even been in a fender bender, much less a major accident, and now she'd witnessed a car driving off a bridge. The stranger's sedan was tipped to one side and the entire hood was crumpled beyond repair.

With shaky hands, Olivia punched in 911, giving the operator as much information as she could remember through her hazy, panic-filled mind. She exited her SUV as she spoke, half running and half sliding down the hill towards the sedan.

When she reached the vehicle and saw the woman inside, her insides churned and she nearly vomited.

Oh, God. Please, no.

Given the height from which the young woman had fallen, could she survive a drop like that?

Was she dead?

In the distance Olivia heard the sound of sirens, but it didn't really register with her. She tried to pry open the driver's side door, but it was half crushed and completely jammed. The car was listing to the right and there was no way she could get to the passenger door.

She yanked again on the driver's door, but it was

wedged shut. She couldn't get it to budge even a little bit.

Not that she would have been much help even if
she could have reached the woman. Olivia had no
medical training, not even in basic first aid. In any
event, the woman's injuries probably stretched far
beyond anything basic first aid could do.

The 911 operator was still on the line with Olivia,
coaching her to stay calm and assuring her help was
on the way. She asked if there were any fluids leaking
from the car, but Olivia didn't think so. If there were,
they were dripping straight into the river.

"Is the person breathing?" the operator asked.

Olivia peered in the window, her gaze focused on
the injured woman, watching for even the slightest
sign of movement. Anything would do. A tremor in
her fingers, the movement of her head, the up and
down movement of the her chest.

Nothing. Icy cold zipped down Olivia's spine.

"I don't know. I don't think so. I can't get the door
open to get to her." Her voice rose as she spoke and
she knew she was approaching complete hysteria.

But maybe the woman was just severely injured.
Maybe—hopefully—the accident wasn't fatal, and
Olivia just didn't know what she should be looking for.

It sure looked fatal.

The sirens grew closer. *Please hurry*, she thought
silently, her pulse pounding in her ears. *Lord, help
this woman.*

"Ma'am? Ma'am?" Olivia knocked on the window
repeatedly. "Ma'am? Can you hear me?"

Nothing.

"First responders are on their way," the telephone

operator assured her. "They've got the necessary equipment to rescue the woman. Please just remain calm and focus on your own breathing."

Focus on *her* breathing? It was the lady in the vehicle who needed help breathing.

The paramedics weren't coming quickly enough. Olivia's gut twisted. She couldn't just stand and do nothing. She had to try again to get to the woman.

But how?

Olivia cupped her hands around her eyes to shade them from the sun's glare and pressed against the window, desperate to discern some sign of life.

Something. Anything.

Please, God.

Nothing.

Her heart pounded as she glanced around the inside of the car. There were several boxes and bags of baby items. Diapers and wipes, baby-boy outfits still in their wrapping, a variety of toys and—

Oh, Lord, be merciful.

An infant car seat. Was there a baby in the car?

Olivia gasped. Another bolt of adrenaline surged through her, stinging every nerve in her body. Her pulse was hammering in her ears, blocking out all other sounds.

She shifted so she was looking in the back window and squinted at the car seat. It took her a moment to be sure, but then she sighed in relief. The five-point harness lay loose and unfastened. Surely if the woman had her baby in the car she would have buckled the dear little child into the seat.

Which brought Olivia back to the poor young lady in question. Was she a mother?

She *hadn't* been wearing a seat belt. It was a wonder she hadn't been ejected from the car. Maybe she didn't have far to travel or thought the back country roads were safe, but it had been a foolish risk not to buckle up.

The sheriff's SUV, followed by a second police vehicle, two fire trucks and an ambulance, arrived, parking next to Olivia's SUV on the road in front of the bridge.

A half dozen firemen poured from the red trucks, gathered their equipment and scrambled down the bank toward the crumpled sedan.

Lucy didn't wait for the firemen to gear up. She shuffled down the slick embankment and jogged straight to Olivia's side, giving her a quick, steadying hug.

A tremor ran through Olivia. She was grateful she lived in a small town where even the sheriff's department was personal.

Lucy left her arm around Olivia's shoulder and kept a firm hand on her elbow, guiding her away from the wreck just as the firemen approached. "Come on, hon," she said gently. "A.J. and the guys will take it from here."

Olivia allowed herself to be led up the embankment toward the flashing lights but hesitated when Lucy escorted her to the ambulance and called one of the paramedics over.

"Hey, Pete. Can you get Olivia a blanket and a bottle of water, please?"

"No—I—" Olivia stammered. She felt cold and her teeth were chattering. "I'm not hurt. The lady in the car needs the paramedics. Don't worry about me. I'll be fine."

"You're in shock," Lucy informed her. "Now let's get you over to your vehicle so you can sit down and gather yourself together."

Lucy accompanied Olivia to her SUV and opened the door for her. Olivia slumped into the driver's seat, clutching the hospital blanket tightly under her chin.

"The woman was driving too fast. A jackrabbit ran into the road. She swerved and…oh, Lord have mercy."

"Right now I just want you to catch your breath and drink your water. I need to get down there and see what I can do to help, but I'd appreciate it if you can stick around until I have the chance to interview you. I don't think you're safe to drive right now, anyway. While you're waiting for me, please try to remember as many details as you possibly can. Are you going to be okay on your own for a moment?"

"Go." Olivia waved her away. "Please. Go help that poor woman."

Olivia opened her water bottle and took a sip, but she couldn't catch her breath as Lucy had instructed. Her lungs burned with the effort.

She watched in a daze as the firefighters carved the door and roof of the vehicle with pneumatic cutters and removed the lifeless woman. They placed her on the gurney the paramedics were holding and covered her with a sheet, even her head.

Olivia shivered. So the young woman was dead, then.

What a tragedy. Tears sprang to Olivia's eyes and

she prayed and wept for the stranger, sobbing until the blanket was soaked with her tears.

More than once, she reached for her phone, her thumb hovering over the first number on her speed dial.

Clint.

He would understand, and oh, how she needed his strong arms around her, comforting her. She desperately wanted to lay her head against the rock-solid wall of his chest and listen to the steady beating of his heart. Maybe then she could get through this.

Would he come if she asked?

Yes. He hid a compassionate heart beneath his gruff exterior. But she didn't just need him now. She needed him for a long time to come.

It frightened her that she wasn't even through the worst of this ordeal yet. Lucy would expect her to relive the whole nightmare and recount everything she could remember about what had happened.

She could do that, but it would be painful. The accident was firmly etched in her mind, and she suspected it would linger for years to come.

The fourth or fifth time she picked up her phone she actually hit the call button but then hastily punched End. Clint had made himself perfectly clear. He didn't want to be a part of her life. No need to burden him with her problems now. She would just have to deal with it herself.

The paramedics removed the body and turned the ambulance back toward town and the Little Horn Regional Medical Center, where the county morgue was located. There was no longer a need for lights and a siren. The woman was beyond anything medicine could do for her.

But the car seat. The clothes. The woman had a baby. She probably had a husband out there somewhere waiting for her to come home.

A baby had just lost his mother.

Olivia thought she was going to be sick. She, maybe more than most, could empathize with the situation. She knew how difficult it had been on the triplets when their father hadn't come home from a rock-climbing day trip.

For over an hour, Lucy and the other members of the sheriff's department searched through the sedan, removing and cataloging papers and bags of baby items. By the time she returned to her, Olivia had managed to collect herself. She was still shaking inside but her body had finally stopped quivering.

"Do you think you can answer a few questions for me back at the station?" the sheriff asked, her gaze full of concern.

"Sure. I'll follow you in, okay?"

Lucy knocked on the roof of Olivia's SUV as a send-off and returned to her own vehicle, cutting the lights and doing a U-turn in order to head back toward Little Horn.

Olivia followed a short distance behind her and ten minutes later pulled into the parking lot at the sheriff's station. She'd never had reason to visit the place before and regretted that she had to do so now.

Her mind was so caught up in what she'd witnessed that she didn't immediately recognize the truck she'd parked next to, but after a moment it sank into her mired consciousness.

Clint. She did a double take, her heart jolting with shock.

What was Clint doing at the sheriff's station? Had he somehow already heard about the accident and that she had been a witness to it? Was he here to support her?

Warmth flooded through her at the thought, chasing away the chill of clinical shock.

Clint was here. She wasn't alone.

With renewed courage, she straightened her shoulders, shed the blanket, folded it over her arm and entered the department.

The receptionist at the front desk was waiting for her and ushered her past the cubicles of various detectives and into Lucy's neat, glass-enclosed office. The entire place was surprisingly loud and much more busy than Olivia would expect in such a small town. Some officers talked and moved from desk to desk. Some hovered over computer screens. Others were tackling what looked like mountains of paperwork.

It took Olivia a moment to absorb it all. There wasn't usually much of note for the sheriff's department to do in Little Horn. Up until the advent of the Robin Hood thieves, the town had had an exceptionally low crime rate. The thieves had kind of ruined that. And now there was this fatal car accident. No wonder the place was buzzing with activity.

She paced the office, waiting for Lucy, who had been waylaid at the front desk, and scanned the outer room. Clint was leaning his hip against Deputy Florenson's desk, his arms crossed and his expression grim.

As if he felt her looking at him, he turned his gaze on

her and his eyes widened. He leaned down and spoke to the deputy and then made a beeline for Lucy's office.

For her.

"Olivia?" He braced his shoulder against the door frame. "I'm surprised to see you here."

"Oh?" Any expectations that he might have been at the station for her benefit were dashed upon the craggy rocks of reality. She slumped into the nearest chair, her legs suddenly weak. "Why are you here?"

His jaw tightened. "I thought you might have heard."

"No. Heard what? I was headed out of town this afternoon and haven't spoken to anyone all day. Did something happen?" As if enough hadn't happened already.

"You could say that." His gaze shifted to somewhere over her left shoulder. "I found my father today."

Olivia stiffened. Clint didn't look particularly happy about the news. She couldn't blame him for being angry, but maybe knowing where the man had disappeared to would give Clint the closure he'd been seeking. Had they had words?

"Where has he been living?" she asked softly, knowing it was a tender subject.

"He hasn't."

"I don't understand."

"Some hikers found a dead body hidden behind some bushes at the base of Cathedral Ridge this morning. Obviously it's decomposed, but they found my father's compass on the body, so there's no doubt."

"And you're positive the compass belonged to your father?"

Clint jerked his chin. "It's engraved."

"Oh, Clint." All thoughts of her own pain and distress immediately fled her mind as her heart and her arms opened to him. She was out of her chair in an instant, enveloping Clint in a hug and holding him tight. "I'm so, so sorry."

It was only then that she realized he wasn't responding as she had expected. He stiffened and clenched his fists at his sides. One beat more and he backed away.

"I—I'm sorry," she said again, and crossed her arms. This time she was apologizing for her mistaken assumptions about their relationship as much as expressing feelings about his father's tragic demise.

"It is what it is," he said gruffly.

She hated that cliché. Life was never as black-and-white as that. "I know you must be feeling overwhelmed right now. I can't even imagine."

"I don't know how I feel." It was as much of an admission from him as she was going to get.

He bent his head and his gaze narrowed on her. "If you didn't hear about my dad, then why are you here?"

The sheriff entered the office before Olivia could respond.

"How are you feeling now?" Lucy asked her. "Are you ready to answer a few questions for me? I promise I'll try to make this as brief and easy on you as I can."

Easy? Nothing about this day was easy.

And the hardest part of all was having Clint standing so near that with one step she could be in his arms.

So close, and yet so very far away.

Never in the history of Little Horn had two major tragedies happened on the same day. The whole town was abuzz with the news. Maggie's Café was overflowing with folks wanting the latest scoop.

Poor Olivia, to have witnessed such a terrible fatal accident. Clint couldn't imagine how she felt right now. For such a sensitive woman to have witnessed something so horrific…

And he'd been so wrapped up in his own problems that he hadn't even noticed how distressed she'd been. He'd treated her abominably. He was ashamed just to think of it.

Olivia had needed to be comforted, and he'd shut himself off and hardened his heart toward her. It was the only way he'd ever learned to handle his feelings, and the myriad emotions pelting him after learning of his father's death were nearly more than he could bear.

He'd shut down. Shoved his feelings deep inside him where no one could see, where he didn't have to deal with them. That was how he'd survived as a foster child. If he didn't care, then no one could hurt him. No one had power over him. Not even the dead.

But in the process, the other day, he'd wounded Olivia. He hadn't been considering her emotions when she'd hugged him. He'd been thinking only about himself.

He wouldn't soon forget the expression on her face when he hadn't responded to her, when he'd stepped away from her embrace.

He hadn't known. If he had, he never would have treated her so shoddily. He would have been there to support her, care for her and lend her his strength, even if he didn't have any left for himself.

He should have been there anyway, whether he'd known something was wrong or not.

For the past two days, he had gone back and forth with himself over whether he should call her to see how she was doing, possibly even use the opportunity to try to explain why he'd been so standoffish at the sheriff's station.

But honestly, he didn't know that she'd even deign to speak to him, and he wouldn't blame her a bit if she didn't.

Too late he'd realized his error. He'd been summarily dismissed from Lucy's office the moment she'd arrived. He'd learned Olivia had witnessed a fatal car accident from others in the department.

Grady Stillwater had been called in to take possession of a letter that was found in the dead woman's belongings, along with an assortment of baby clothes, toys and a car seat.

Speculation within the department abounded, although folks were cautioned not to speak of it beyond the doors of the sheriff's station.

Was this Cody's mother? Had she come to town to finally make things right with Ben Stillwater, Grady's identical twin brother and the father of the child?

Poor guy. Grady had told Clint that Ben wasn't in a good place right now, what with the painful and slow-going physical therapy he had to endure. Relearning the basics—eating, speaking, fine motor skills. He was understandably frustrated with the process. While Clint and Ben hadn't exactly been friends, that didn't stop Clint's concern. Ben had been an active man before the accident, and Clint hated how much he'd withered away.

The deceased woman's letter had been delivered into Grady's hands, and after days of uncertainty, he had decided to pass it to his brother, asking Clint to accompany him to the hospital. The veteran didn't say it out loud, but Clint knew he wanted moral support while delivering what could be a very excruciating letter to his ailing brother.

Clint and Grady had been friends all their lives, so Clint had always favored his side of things. Grady had resented Ben, and the brothers had fought constantly.

Now Grady was trying to mend fences. Clint was glad to support him, even if he hadn't always agreed with the way Ben had lived his life. The man used to have a wild, narcissistic lifestyle, thinking only of himself.

But that was before the accident. Now he had a baby. Clint hoped that would settle him down. A father needed to be there for his family.

Who was Clint to judge? He certainly couldn't throw the first stone.

Grady hadn't opened the letter. He said he imagined it was probably personal and he didn't want to pry, especially because he was trying so hard to repair the relationship with his brother.

Clint couldn't begin to guess how Ben would accept the news that Cody's mother had died, never mind absorbing whatever had ultimately become her last words to him. According to Grady, Ben was still struggling to wrap his mind around the fact that he was suddenly a father. Their grandmother, Mamie Stillwater, had brought Baby Cody to the hospital a few times so Ben could interact with him, but Ben still tired easily.

It would be a long and sometimes painful process for him to heal—for the family to heal. Clint prayed the Stillwaters would finally find the peace they deserved.

Once at the hospital, Grady killed the engine of his truck and glanced over at Clint and tried to smile, but Clint could see how difficult it was for him.

"Are you ready?" Clint asked.

"Not in this lifetime." Grady groaned. "It's gotta be done, though. Ben has the right to know what happened to the mother of his baby. I might as well get it over with."

Clint nodded and clapped Grady's shoulder.

"Thanks for coming along."

"You got it, bud."

When they reached Ben's floor, Grady hesitated before the door. He took a deep breath and threaded his fingers through his hair before walking into the room, his limp still slightly noticeable.

His friend's expression was laced with pain, but Clint wasn't certain whether it was because of the physical injury he'd sustained in war or emotional pain caused by the rift and enmity between the two brothers.

Grady pressed his palm over his shirt pocket.

The letter.

How would Ben receive it?

Grady took another deep breath and schooled his features. He greeted his brother with an upbeat smile, but Ben only grunted in response. His speech was slowly returning, but apparently he didn't care to practice his skills on Grady. He was clenching his jaw as a male physical therapist worked on one of his legs.

Grady winced. Clint knew his friend likewise had a long road of physical therapy ahead of him. In that the two brothers could not be more the same—although Grady had gone and fallen in love with his physical therapist, Chloe Miner. They were now engaged and would be married soon.

Clint had no doubt that Ben would get back on his feet. He was a strong man with a personality to match, and now he had an even bigger and better reason to recover: his son.

Clint felt as if he was an equally painfully slow learner, discovering all too late the value of family, now that he'd thrown away the possibility of being a part of the one family he cared about more than anything.

The Barlows.

"What's up, bro?" Ben asked through gritted teeth, concentrating on the movements the physical therapist was performing. "Everything okay at the ranch?"

Grady paused. Clint wondered if Ben caught his brother's hesitation, but he didn't appear to notice. Clint was aware of it only because he knew about the explosive letter Grady carried in his pocket.

"How's Mamie? And my son?"

"They're well. Mamie and Chloe will be by later today with Cody."

"That's good."

The physical therapist helped Ben into a sitting position and admonished him to remember to get up and walk as much as possible.

Ben groaned as soon as the man left. "That guy is a slave driver. I gotta tell you, brother, you have it easy. Chloe is a good sight better on the eyes."

Grady chuckled. "But no less of a dictator. She's as tough as nails when it comes to her work. She doesn't give an inch."

Ben laughed and propped himself up on his elbows. "Yeah, but she loves you. You've caught yourself a good one."

Grady's lips curved up. "Don't I know it!"

"You'd better be treating her right, because if I find out otherwise, I'm coming after you."

"I'd like to see you try."

Ben laughed, then winced and laid his head back on his pillow.

Grady's brow scrunched over his nose. He was immediately at Ben's side, supporting his brother's back and elbow until he was comfortably situated.

"Do you want your bed adjusted higher? Should I call a nurse?"

"Don't hover," Ben demanded, but even Clint could see how pale and gaunt he looked. Everything was white except his cheeks, which were a flaming red. His sandy-blond hair was slicked back from sweat. His pupils were dilated and his eyelids were drooping with exhaustion. Clint didn't need a doctor to know Ben needed to rest.

"You look beat," Grady said, his voice husky. He covered him with a blanket and tucked it around his sides. "Get some rest. You'll want to be fresh for Mamie and little Cody."

"Yeah," Ben agreed, already fading. "Little Cody."

Grady met Clint's gaze and jerked his head toward the door. Clint, his hands stuffed in the pockets of his jeans jacket, followed him out into the hallway.

"That didn't go as well as I had hoped," Grady said in a low voice.

"He's doing better though, right? I'm sure it's going to take some time for him to heal."

Grady glanced down at his bum leg. "Yeah."

"You know that better than anyone. He'll get there. He's nothing if not stubborn."

"He doesn't have the support system I had. I don't know what I would have done without Chloe. Her encouragement has made all the difference for me."

Clint's heart clenched. He would never have that kind of support because he hadn't given it. He almost envied Grady and Ben. Their injuries, however terrible, were physical. Doctors and physical therapists could help them heal. And they had each other to lean on.

He had no one. And there was no medicine to heal a broken heart.

"Ben won't be doing this alone," Grady vowed. "I'm going to be beside him every step of the way. He's due to get out of the hospital here in a few days and I plan to be there right alongside him for as long as he needs me."

Clint nodded. "Of course you will. Ben's blessed to have you for a brother."

Grady frowned. "He probably doesn't think so. We've been at each other's throats for most of our adult lives."

"Things are different now."

"I can't believe I'm saying this, but I think they are. I'm hopeful." Grady patted his shirt pocket. "I just pray this letter doesn't mess it all up. Ben's been through enough. You saw how ragged and worn-out he looked."

"He's probably just having a bad day. You know how it goes when your body is healing. You take two steps forward, one step back."

And with a healing heart, it was one step forward, two steps back.

"Ben deserves to know the truth," Grady said with renewed vigor. "The whole truth. If that woman is— was—Cody's mother, Ben needs to know what happened to her. There won't ever be any closure for him if he believes the baby's mother could still be out there somewhere."

Clint nodded. He knew how painful it was to live without closure. Even though he was going to have to bury his father, at least now he knew the truth. Dad hadn't abandoned him. He was with the Lord, and someday, God willing, Clint would be happily reunited with him.

Clint's cell phone rang just as they reached Grady's pickup. It was Lucy Benson calling from the sheriff's station.

"Excuse me just a moment," he told Grady. "It's the sheriff. I need to take this, if you don't mind."

"Take your time." Grady frowned, concern etching his brow, and waved him on. He knew about Clint's dad and that Clint was waiting for forensics to settle on when and how the man had died.

Clint no longer needed to know. He just wanted to be done with it. To move on.

If he could move on. Without Olivia and the boys it was a disheartening notion.

"Sheriff?" he answered. "What's up?"

Lucy cut right to the chase. "Forensics has determined that there was very little blunt force trauma to the body. Your father did sustain one possibly fatal blow to his head, the size of the injury consistent with that of a rock."

"Only one? So he didn't fall climbing Cathedral Ridge, then?" For some reason Clint was relieved by the news. His father hadn't done something foolish, after all.

"It's doubtful. All we can do is speculate at this point, but we suspect he may have accidentally come upon a rattlesnake's nest. If he'd been bitten several times, he might have been shocked enough to fall and hit his head on a rock."

Clint's heart felt like lead. His poor father.

Guilt washed over him for all the years he'd thought terrible things about the man, only to find out he'd died in a tragic accident. It was almost too much for Clint to handle. He bunched the fabric of his black T-shirt in his fist.

"I'm sorry we can't be more specific," Lucy told him. "But we can release his body to you now, whenever you're ready for it."

"Pastor John has been helping me with the arrangements. We can lay him to rest right away. I'm not planning a funeral service or anything."

"Okay. That will be fine. And Clint? Again, I just want to say how sorry I am for your loss."

He sighed deeply. "Thanks, Lucy. I appreciate all you've done for me and Dad."

"Anytime."

Just as he clicked off the phone, it vibrated again. Expecting that Lucy had forgotten to tell him something, he answered without looking at the identity of the caller.

"Clint?" Olivia sobbed into the phone.

His breath caught as he gripped the device close to his ear. "Olivia? What's wrong?"

Her breaths were coming short and fast and were peppered with high, piercing hiccups of distress.

"It's the boys," she cried.

"What? What's wrong with the triplets?" *Oh, no, Lord. Not the boys.* Clint could handle almost anything, but not anything having to do with Olivia and her sons.

"Oh, Clint. They're gone."

"What do you mean, gone?" He opened the passenger side door of Grady's truck and gestured for him to start the engine. Then he cupped his hand over the receiver and spoke hastily to his friend. "Can you take me to Barlow Acres? There's an emergency."

"I'm on it," Grady said, reaching for the ignition.

"Olivia?" Clint said into the phone. It was so still and silent on the other end he was afraid he might have somehow lost reception. "Are you there?"

She whimpered. "They left a note for me," she explained in a tight voice. "They took their horses and went into the Deep Gulch Mountains."

Clint's gut somersaulted and he thought he might be sick right then and there. He put his hand over the receiver again.

"Can you take me home instead?" he asked Grady. He needed to get his dog and his horse.

Oh, Lord, help us.

"Did they say why?"

"They're looking for your treasure."

There was no blame or censure in her tone, but there should have been. Clint felt as if he'd been slapped.

He'd screwed up. Again. He'd royally messed with other people's lives, and now three little boys were in danger because of him.

"I'll find them," he said, struggling to keep the edge out of his voice. He needed to remain calm for her, even though he was feeling anything but. "Olivia, I promise on my last breath that I will find your sons and bring them home to you."

"Take me with you," she begged. "Please. I can't just sit here not knowing."

He paused, vacillating on his decision. She'd slow him down. The boys already had a head start on them. He didn't know how long they'd been gone, but every second counted in an emergency.

And yet how could he say no to a mother in distress? How could he cause Olivia even a moment's pain beyond what she'd already endured?

"Stay put," he told her. "I'm on my way."

Chapter Ten

Olivia hung up the phone and stared out the front window, her pulse ticking off the seconds. Every minute that she waited, her boys were getting farther away. The deeper into the Deep Gulch Mountains they went, the more chances they had of falling into danger or getting completely and hopelessly lost. Even an experienced mountain man like Clint's father had run into tragedy in Deep Gulch. Her boys were only six.

Her heart clenched. The triplets would be so frightened if they got lost.

Mending fences on the far side of her property, she'd only missed the school bus by a few minutes, and the boys knew to get themselves a snack and stay put until she returned to the house. It was just like Caleb, Levi and Noah to get some crazy notion into their heads and then pursue it without thinking things all the way through. Among the three of them, they often egged each other on to more and more mischief. But this one took the cake.

Lord, please watch over them. Help them remember all Clint taught them about wilderness safety.

They knew how to bridle their own horses but weren't big enough to saddle them yet, so they'd taken off riding bareback. They were good riders, especially for their age, but some of the trails in Deep Gulch were treacherous for even more experienced riders.

The more she thought about it, the more worried she became. She didn't know where Clint was when she'd called him, but if he'd been at home she was positive he would have arrived by now.

Had he already been in the mountains when she'd called? She'd insisted he come back to get her without even thinking about where he was when she'd asked.

How foolish. She should have trusted him to go without her, let him do what he knew best, search and rescue, without her interference.

She watched the second hand of her kitchen clock tick slowly around. One minute. Two.

She couldn't wait any longer. Her entire being was screaming for action. Her boys were in jeopardy. Clint could catch up with her.

The mental picture of Clint's father lying dead and unnoticed for over twenty years grated through her like metal on metal.

She tried Clint's cell number several times but it went straight to voice mail, so she dashed off a note to him and taped it to the front door. He'd probably be furious with her for not waiting for him, but it couldn't be helped.

After tying a sweatshirt around her waist, she filled a backpack with granola bars, fruit and water bottles. She moved on instinct. The rest of the world was hazy, but her priority thoughts crystal clear. She had to find her boys.

Not bothering with a saddle, she bridled Cimarron and swung her leg over the mare's back, urging her into a gallop as soon as they cleared the barn door.

She rode toward the mountains the way crows flew, bypassing most of the county roads and taking every shortcut she knew of and even some she didn't.

The mountain range was enormous. Where would her sons think to go?

They might have done just what she had and aimed their horses for the nearest peak. If they'd given their horses their heads there was no telling where they might be.

On the other hand, Noah especially was remarkably good at directions. He could often tell her where they were headed just by which route she was driving the vehicle. It was logical to assume that they might have decided to follow the Pine Meadow Trail, the same one they'd taken when they'd accompanied Clint on their day trip.

She reached the base of the mountains and reined in, considering her alternatives.

She should have waited for Clint. He was experienced. He'd have known what to do, where to start looking. And he had Pav to help him.

She'd been mistaken to leave too soon.

But it was too late to go back now. Clint had probably already received her note and was now on his way. At this point, backtracking wouldn't help her— or her sons.

Deciding to follow her gut instinct, she turned her horse toward the Pine Meadow trailhead.

* * *

Clint slid off his gelding and ran up onto Olivia's porch three steps at a time. He was surprised she wasn't waiting out front with her mare already saddled. It had taken him longer than he'd anticipated getting back to James and Libby's ranch, even though Grady had done his best. Then Clint had had to saddle his gelding and get Pav prepared for the journey.

Clint rang the doorbell but no one answered. He opened the screen door to knock and a piece of paper fluttered down onto his boots.

Clint—
I'm sorry. I couldn't wait any longer. Please hurry.
Olivia

Oh, Lord, please help me. What has she done?

Had she put herself in danger going out to look for the boys? She hadn't even told him where she was going. It was bad enough that the triplets were missing. Now Olivia, as well?

He growled in frustration. He was angry with her, but at the same time, he knew he would have done the exact same thing if it had been his kids who were missing.

Which was precisely what it felt like to him right now—as if the triplets were his own children. The love he felt in his heart for them was undeniable. The sheer sense of panic that threatened to overwhelm him when he thought of never seeing them again was terrifying.

As for Olivia—he couldn't even begin to put his feelings for Olivia into any sort of order.

They were his family. And he'd let them down.

Even now it might be too late.

No.

That was *so* not going to happen.

He ran down to the barn with Pav right on his heels. As he expected, the boys' horses were gone, and so was Olivia's mare.

He let Pav sniff around for a moment while he searched for something belonging to the boys or Olivia, something to give Pav the extra lead he needed.

Desperate, Clint searched every nook and cranny, at first finding nothing and then suddenly spying a piece of cloth stuffed behind a bale of hay.

Praying, he snatched at the piece of clothing. It was one of the boys' navy blue T-shirts, ripped down the center from the neck. Either they'd thrown it into the barn to use as a rag or one of his muggles was trying to hide a mistake from their mama's stern attention.

Clint didn't care either way. It was the break he'd been looking for.

"C'mon, Pav. Let's find our family."

He mounted up and galloped down the country road, heading straight toward the Pine Meadow trailhead. Pav didn't gallivant around as he usually did, but rather stayed right on the horse's heels.

Clint's mind was buzzing with facts and questions. The boys were smart. If they were indeed searching for Clint's treasure, they'd follow the path from where they started their day trip together—assuming they could find the place. It's what he would have done.

He had to pray he was right. He wouldn't even think of the alternative.

As for Olivia, he had no idea where she had gone. Had she come to the same conclusion he had about starting at the Pine Meadow Trail?

He hoped so, for all their sakes. And he prayed that since he knew the route so well, he could gain precious time on her and overtake her. Together they could search for the triplets.

He was fairly certain she, at least, would stay on the marked trail, unless she had a very good reason to venture from it, and then she wouldn't go very far.

The boys he was not so sure about. How much would six-year-olds remember of what he'd taught them about wilderness survival on a single day hike?

Enough to keep them safe and together, he hoped. Clint bent over his gelding's neck and let him have his head.

Lord, keep the Barlows safe.

It was all Clint could think of to pray. Doubt clouded his mind. So much could go wrong. There were too many variables, and the Deep Gulch range covered hundreds of miles.

It could eat three little boys whole, and no one would know for sure where they'd gone. Like his father, they—

No.

He would not think that way. Someone knew where the boys were, and He would take care of them.

God.

Lord, give me guidance.

The sky didn't open. There were no bright lights or stars pointing the way. But suddenly Clint's search and rescue training kicked in, calming his frantic thoughts and emotions.

He needed to stay focused for Olivia and the triplets' sake. Think and pray. Their lives depended on it.

And he would not let them down.

Chapter Eleven

Olivia was lost.

She was lost, and it wasn't until she'd completely veered off the known path she'd been following that she realized she was going in circles. The third time she came upon the same shallow pond, she knew she'd made a mistake.

But there was always her cell phone.

Clint thought she was a muggle, as he'd called it, where treasure hunting was concerned, and maybe she was. At the moment she was hunting the greatest treasure of them all—her sons—and she would not fail them.

She might not be an expert like Clint was, but she could use a GPS as well as the next woman. This was the twenty-first century, after all. She'd punch in her home address and *bam*, she'd know which direction to go.

Then it was just a matter of finding a hiking trail or breaking into a clearing. Once she got her bearings, she would be fine. How hard could it be?

She just needed to keep calm and…

Where was her phone?

She always carried it with her in the back left pocket of her jeans. Always. Had it slipped out somewhere during her wild bareback gallop or—

Oh, no.

She'd set it down on the kitchen table when she was writing the note to Clint. She could picture it sitting there, glinting up at her. How had she forgotten to double-check such an important detail?

How could she be so stupid?

Her breaths became shallow and she felt so light-headed that she reined Cimarron to a halt and slid off her back. That was all Olivia needed, to pass out and fall off her horse. The last thing she wanted was to injure herself right now.

She was well and truly lost, with no cell phone and nothing more than water bottles and a couple snacks to sustain her.

Worse yet, her *boys* were out there somewhere, also without cell phones and with no way to contact the outside world.

If only she'd waited for Clint.

He was probably fuming right now. She'd called him back into her life in the worst of circumstances, expecting him to ride in and save the day.

And then she'd left without him.

But wasn't that what Clint did? Save people?

Just thinking of his face calmed her down a little bit, at least enough for her to tether her sweat-lathered mare and drop cross-legged underneath a tall cypress tree.

She bowed her head and prayed for wisdom and guidance. She'd gotten herself into this mess by going off half-cocked and without considering her actions through to their logical conclusions. She'd acted first and then thought about it.

So she'd have to get herself out by doing the exact opposite—thinking first and then acting. It was especially important for her to remain calm and rational right now, even if her pulse was still pounding in her head.

What would Clint do?

She couldn't remember. She'd spent as much time admiring his rugged profile as she had actually listening to all he'd been teaching her sons about wilderness survival. Perhaps she should have paid a little more attention to his words instead of his smile.

Let's see…

She remembered him giving each of the boys a whistle. Well, that was no help. She didn't have a whistle on her, and she'd never been able to master whistling with her lips, either—at least not the kind of piercing sound she'd need to catch anyone's attention. The best she could do was whistle a tune, and that wasn't going to help.

What else?

She'd brought food and water, which was good thinking, but she was saving that for the boys. Besides, at the moment she couldn't eat if her life depended on it, which thankfully was not the case. Yet. Her stomach was churning like a combine threshing wheat.

It hadn't even occurred to her that *she* could get lost—which just went to show her how foolish she'd been. She hadn't packed a single thing for her own needs.

If—*when*—Clint found her, she would willingly turn around and allow him to kick her behind for being such an idiot.

What about that girl he said he'd rescued? Betsy McKay? He'd praised her for something she'd done when she'd gotten lost while hiking. What was it?

Olivia scowled, trying to remember.

Oh, that's right. She'd stayed in one place and hadn't let herself get flustered.

That was difficult advice to follow. Every nerve ending in Olivia's body was alight with panic. It couldn't be much past noon, but the sun would set eventually and then it would get cold. Freezing cold.

That alone made her want to mount back up on Cimarron and just ride. She could at least try to find her own way out of the woods. Surely she'd come upon a legitimate hiking trail sooner or later.

Or she could just keep riding in circles and get nowhere fast. She had no way to know.

Suddenly she saw the wisdom behind the sage advice. She should stay where she was and wait to be rescued. But that didn't make it any easier. She wasn't a stay-and-wait-to-be-rescued kind of woman. She prided herself on her independence, even when it got her into trouble.

And it didn't help to know her sons were also out there somewhere, probably more lost and frightened than she was. If nothing else, she wanted to keep moving for that reason alone.

Lord, take care of my boys. Help Clint find them.

"I will."

Olivia jumped to her feet so quickly she hit her head on a low-hanging branch. She hadn't realized she had prayed aloud. She whirled toward that oh-so-familiar deep voice, her heart warming even before she made contact with his gorgeous hazel eyes.

Clint.

"Clint!" She launched herself at him, grasping his shoulders and pulling him out of the saddle. "Oh, thank God. Thank God."

"Definitely. I'm not taking credit for what the good Lord has done today."

Pav ran around her legs, barking and licking her hand. She laughed and scratched the golden retriever's ears, then wrapped her arms around Clint's neck and hugged him tight.

"You found me. You found me." She was aware that she was repeating every statement she made, but she couldn't seem to help herself. She was just so elated to see him.

He chuckled. "Of course I found you. It's my job, remember? Search and rescue?"

His job. Of course.

She backed off, feeling as if he'd thrown cold water on her.

"I'm sorry. I shouldn't have wandered off the trail. And then I discovered I accidentally left my cell phone at home and—" She shifted gears without finishing her statement. "Did you find the boys?"

He scowled and shook his head. "I had to make a detour to find you first. I followed the Pine Meadow Trail until I saw a recent disturbance in the grass. Then I followed your tracks fairly easily. Why did you leave the trail, anyway? Even if you got nothing else out of our day trip together you should have at least remembered that much."

She didn't like that he was scolding her as if she were a schoolgirl, but she supposed she deserved it. She tipped her chin up and looked right at him. He could castigate her all he wanted once everyone was home safely. Right now they needed to find the boys.

"I was positive I heard laughter. I followed the sound. I called and I called for the triplets but couldn't find them. Then I looked around and realized I was lost."

"It happens easily in the mountains." He pressed his lips together. "You and I had the same idea about where the boys might be going." Olivia was relieved to see that his head was back in the game. "Do you think they could have found the trailhead on their own?"

"Yes. Noah is very perceptive about directions. I'm sure he wouldn't have any trouble getting back here."

"Good. That's good. We're on the right track, then. We just need to find them now."

She hoped they were on the right track. They simply *had* to be.

"Follow me. We'll backtrack to the trail and then follow it on in. You said you thought you heard them laughing. Pav and I came across your trail first. The boys could be just a little farther down the trail."

Clint scooped up her backpack and slung it over his shoulder, then mounted his gelding and waited for her to mount Cimarron.

Pav barked and ran in circles. Clint turned his horse and she followed. He didn't speak to her. She didn't know if that was because he was angry with her or whether it was because he was picking his way back to the trail and was scanning the area for signs that the boys had been there.

Maybe both.

She didn't say anything because she didn't want to bother him when he was working. And because she was ashamed of herself for making things so much more difficult for him.

If the boys were hurt because Clint had had to take precious time out to find her she would never forgive herself. In trying to help them she might have done just the opposite.

Clint turned in his saddle and caught her eyes with his intense gaze. "Don't."

She pulled up. What had she done now? She looked around but couldn't see any markings she might have disturbed. Had she accidentally trodden over some important clue?

"Don't what?"

"Don't blame yourself. This isn't your fault."

"How did you—?"

"You're thinking so loud I can hear you from clear up here."

"You cannot." She clicked her tongue against her teeth. He couldn't read minds, but he was making a concerted effort to make her feel better, which she appreciated more than he would ever know. She'd never be able to pay him back for this. Not ever.

"Okay, well, maybe I can't hear your thoughts, but I know you well enough to know that your sons are everything to you. And you're a single mother. If something goes wrong, it's usually all on you."

Her shoulders dropped. He really did know her. She'd shared with him the struggles she'd gone through as a single parent. The cold, hard truth of the matter was that it *would* be entirely her fault if something terrible happened to her kids. There was no passing the buck here.

He reined his gelding in a half circle and nudged him forward and alongside Cimarron until he and Olivia were facing each other and their knees were nearly touching. He reached for her hand.

"It's not, you know." His voice was low and husky.

"Not what?" She wasn't following.

"It's not all on you now. I'm here to share the burden."

Tears sprang to her eyes. She'd been alone for so long that to have Clint come alongside her this way left her speechless.

And grateful.

She tried to express her gratitude, to let him know how much his words meant to her, but despite her best efforts, nothing came out of her mouth.

He smiled and squeezed her hand and then gently brushed the tears from her cheek with the pad of his thumb. "Don't cry, sweetheart, and don't worry. We're going to find them. You've got smart kids. They're fine. You just wait. By this evening we'll all be laughing at—"

He was interrupted by the shrill peal of one, and then two, and then three sharp whistles.

The triplets had good heads on their shoulders. Clint couldn't have been prouder of them if they were his own children.

And he couldn't have been more relieved when he and Olivia came upon the three boys, who were chattering excitedly about something and seemed completely oblivious to the fact that they were lost.

Or maybe they weren't lost at all. They had stayed on the marked path and had cut straight into the meadow where they'd shared the picnic lunch with Clint the last time they'd been in Deep Gulch. They'd even brought a blanket to spread out on the grass.

They'd used the whistles Clint had given them but didn't appear to be in any kind of distress. Between the boys shouting and Pav barking it was hard to tell *what* was going on.

Clint was going to ask, but Olivia jumped in before he could speak.

"*What* do you boys think you were doing, taking off into the mountains by yourselves? You scared us half to death."

His heart warmed. Olivia had, whether consciously or unconsciously, included him in the picture. She'd said *us*.

For all her scolding, she slipped off her horse and enveloped all three boys in a big bear hug.

Caleb's blond eyebrows dropped in confusion. "But Mama, we left you a note and told you where we were going. Did we spell something wrong?"

"No, honey. I understood your note. But you know better than to go riding off on your own without supervision. You could have been hurt. All three of you are grounded for a week. No video games. No television. And you can't play with the ducklings."

The boys seemed to take losing their television privileges in stride, but their faces fell at the mention of their ducklings.

"But Mama," whined Levi, "our duckies will starve

if we don't feed them. You said we had to be responstible for them, remember? That we had to feed them every day no matter what?"

Olivia smothered a laugh and a sob at the same time. Clint had no idea what to do with that.

"Why did you whistle?" he asked curiously, dismounting and leaving his gelding to graze. "It doesn't look like you found yourself in any kind of trouble."

Except for being grounded, Clint thought with amusement. His relief at finding the boys made him feel giddy, as if a weight had been lifted from him. He could breathe again.

"We whistled so you could find us," Noah said matter-of-factly. It apparently hadn't occurred to the boys that Clint and Olivia would not immediately follow them into Deep Gulch, and yet they hadn't even considered the fact that they might get in trouble for just that.

"We couldn't wait," Caleb continued. "Because we found the treasure!"

"What?" Olivia exclaimed, for the moment apparently completely forgetting that the boys weren't supposed to be up here in the first place. "What do you mean, you found the treasure? Where is it?"

"Did not," Levi said, shoving Caleb. One look from Olivia stopped that behavior dead in its tracks.

"So did you or didn't you find the treasure?" Olivia asked, to clarify. She lifted an eyebrow.

"Yes," said Caleb.

"No," said Levi.

"Kinda," said Noah. All eyes turned on him. "Not the treasure, exactly," he continued. "But we know what part of the riddle means."

Clint crouched before Noah. "Okay, buddy. What have you got?"

Noah turned and pointed to Cathedral Ridge towering just a short distance away.

Clint shook his head. "I'm not getting it. What do you see? What are you trying to show me?"

"A face," exclaimed Caleb and Levi together, all sibling rivalry set aside, for the moment at least.

"See?" said Levi, pointing. "It's a man. He's lying down. There is his eye and an eyebrow," he announced triumphantly. "And he has a big nose and look at his mouth. See? He's smiling."

Come to think of it, the peak of Cathedral Ridge did vaguely resemble an old man's nose. If Clint squinted, he could make out a face. Kind of.

How had he missed something so obvious? Because he wasn't paying attention? It had been right in front of him all along and yet he'd overlooked it again and again. It had taken a trio of bright six-year-olds to make the find for him.

"'Joy watches over,'" Olivia whispered in awe. "Well, you can just go ahead and knock me down with a feather. Clint, I think the boys might be right."

"That's where they found my dad," he agreed. "But they didn't find any treasure. They swept the place clean, and you know how thorough the sheriff is."

"Yes, but—"

"I already asked. I wish there was something there, but there just isn't."

"Maybe they missed something," Olivia said thoughtfully, unwilling to drop the subject. "Was your dad planning to bury your treasure?"

"I think so."

"The sheriff's department wouldn't have been looking for that, would they?" Her voice was growing more and more excited with every word. "And they didn't have the riddle."

"Even if we've solved the second half of the riddle, and I grant you it's likely the boys are right. we're still left with trying to figure out the first part. What does 'Three grows into one' mean?"

She nibbled on her bottom lip. It was distracting. How was he supposed to think through a riddle when she was doing that? Now that Olivia and the boys were safe, his attention kept wandering toward her, and the whole biting-her-bottom-lip thing wasn't helping.

"I have no idea," she said at last.

"We should probably start heading back," Clint said. He was reluctant to end the afternoon, especially when he didn't know what the future held for him in regard to the Barlows. Would everything go back to the way it had been? Would he no longer be welcome in their lives?

"What?" Olivia exclaimed, reaching for his shoulder. "You want to leave when we're so close to finding your treasure? Surely all this couldn't be for nothing."

He didn't care about the treasure anymore. He had all he wanted right here in front of him. Olivia and the triplets—*they* were his treasure.

But the boys' eyes were gleaming with anticipation and even Olivia was looking at him expectantly.

He sighed dramatically, as if he were being put upon to concede to their demands. In truth it was actually the opposite. He was ready to beg to spend more time with them.

"Okay," he concurred. "We can take a look around. But we can't stay too late. I want us all back home before the sun sets."

"Agreed," Olivia said immediately. "Whatever you say. You're the expert."

Clint snorted and rolled his eyes. As if she'd ever really listened to him when he was spouting his *expert* advice. "Yeah, right."

Olivia ignored his sarcasm. "Where do you think we should look first?"

He laughed. "How should I know? I missed the obvious answer to the second half of the riddle and I've been looking for twenty-six years. Anyway, you're the one leading this particular expedition, with all your cocaptains here. I'm just along for the ride."

"By the rocks! By the rocks!" the triplets exclaimed in unison.

"I'm not sure that's a good idea," Clint said, thinking of his father—and the triplets' father, as well. "It's not safe over there. I don't want the boys anywhere near that ridge."

"What if we only went as far as the clearing?" Olivia suggested. "That won't be dangerous, will it?"

"I suppose we can do that. I doubt we'll find anything, though."

Olivia grinned at him. "Then you don't know my boys. If the treasure is there, they'll find it."

They mounted up and Clint led them on toward Cathedral Ridge. He'd take them as far as the clearing where the trees edged the grassland around the base of the ridge and then he would take the Barlows home.

He was *so* done looking for treasure. He'd been so preoccupied with that stupid pursuit that, just as he'd missed seeing the face on the mountain, he'd nearly missed the *real* treasures of his heart—and they had been right in front of his nose all along.

Ten minutes later they broke into the clearing.

"Stay with your mother and me," Clint cautioned. He knew he was being overprotective and that the boys were fine, but after everything that had happened recently, he couldn't seem to help himself.

He let the boys trot around for a while. A couple times they got distracted playing games with Pav and their horses. Clint caught himself laughing at their antics, and more than once he and Olivia shared knowing smiles.

She didn't seem to want to talk and he couldn't think of anything to say that wouldn't lead to him putting both feet in his mouth. He was bound to blurt out something like "I can't live without you" or "How do you feel about me becoming the triplets' insta-daddy?" Yeah, that would go over well. He popped a piece of spearmint gum in his mouth and concentrated on chewing it.

After about half an hour he called the boys in, ignoring the collective groans.

"Okay, guys," he said, after they'd pulled their horses into a loose circle. "It's time to go now."

"No, wait," Levi squealed, surprising his horse so much it bucked forward and nearly unseated him. But like a true horseman, and despite riding bareback, Levi compensated and stayed on.

"Look," he said in a softer but no less animated voice. He pointed toward a thicket of trees in the distance. "I see it. 'Three grows into one.'"

Chapter Twelve

Olivia looked in the direction Levi was pointing and gasped. She saw it, too. She flicked her gaze toward Clint to see if he also recognized what Levi was talking about. The answer to Clint's riddle was right in front of them.

Three enormous, strangely deformed trees had grown together, their trunks and limbs intertwined in what looked like some peculiar piece of modern art.

"Let's go look," she suggested, but the boys had already nudged their horses into a trot. Picking up on the excitement, Pav ran back and forth between the boys and Clint and Olivia, baying and chasing his tail.

"Your barking tenor sounds like a bass," Olivia teased.

Clint clicked his tongue and nudged his gelding into a canter. He easily passed the triplets and reached the oddly shaped trees first. By the time he'd dismounted, the boys had reached him, and together they went to investigate the area.

Olivia's heart was firmly lodged in her throat, and not just because they were about to find a treasure that was twenty-six years in the making. She knew how much it meant to Clint and she was glad for him, but what was choking her up was the gentle, joyful way in which he interacted with her sons. Here he was about to finally put a painful memory to rest and yet his attention appeared to be more focused on the boys than any treasure they might find.

How could she possibly walk away from him when all this was over?

She slid off Cimarron just as Clint and the boys leaned forward, their heads in a semicircle.

"Well, I'll be a monkey's uncle," Clint said, taking off his hat and running his palm back over his hair before he replaced it and pushed the rim down over his eyes. "Come look, Olivia. It's here. It's really here."

His voice was getting husky, and empathetic tears sprang to Olivia's eyes. She knew what this moment meant to him. And she was glad. So happy for him.

"I can't believe it." He braced his forearm against his thigh and stared down at the bowl-like crevice created by the intertwined tree trunks. "After all this time. Come on, my muggles. Pull it out for me."

The boys scrambled around him, squealing with excitement. Olivia was curious as to what the treasure looked like.

"Can you guys reach it?" Clint asked.

"Wait," Olivia said, holding up a cautionary hand. The boys stopped and looked at her. "Clint, don't you think you ought to be the one to do the honors? It's your treasure, after all. You've spent so much time and energy trying to find it. It only seems fair."

"It's not mine," Clint countered, shaking his head.

"It's ours. I wouldn't ever have found this without the boys solving the riddle for me. I *want* the triplets to open the box and see what's inside." He removed the little silver key from around his neck.

With the three boys and Clint all begging her with puppy dog looks that could have rivaled Pav's, she finally capitulated. She still thought Clint should open the box, but it was his decision to make, and he apparently wanted the boys to help.

The triplets lifted a rectangular, burgundy-colored metal lockbox out of the hole, although twenty-six years of overgrowth from the trees made it more complicated than it might have been otherwise.

The boys took turns trying to open the box, but the latch was rusted shut. Clint picked up a small stone and used it like a hammer. It took him only two strokes to break the lock.

Olivia held her breath and watched Clint's face as the boys reverently opened the box. There was sadness in his features, but also joy. And when he saw what was inside, his smile could have lit up every star in a midnight sky.

"I can't believe it," he breathed as the triplets held up a rocket, complete with a launcher, and carefully packaged in layers of plastic. He swiped the back of his hand across his brow. Olivia thought he might have been surreptitiously dashing away a tear. "I always wanted one of these. I begged my dad for one, but he always said I was too young to have it. I can't believe—" His voice broke and he ran a hand down his face. "He didn't forget."

Olivia moved to Clint's side and put her arm around

his shoulder. "He loved you," she murmured, allowing Clint a moment for the reality to set in. "Your dad really loved you."

Everything in Clint's life had come down to this moment.

When he was a child, his world had been torn apart in an instant. Moving from foster home to foster home had taught him to trust nothing and no one.

He'd carried the burden of anger and resentment for too long. The Everharts had poured their love on him and he'd respected them for that, but he'd believed it had come too late for him to change the cynical man he'd become.

He still didn't know how beautiful Olivia and her three lively sons had somehow broken through the barriers he'd erected, and had edged their way into his heart. She'd given him new faith—in God and in people.

And yet still he'd backed away. He'd believed he was broken beyond repair. Discovering his father had not abandoned him was another game changer for him, shifting his whole worldview. And then this treasure, this final gift from his dad, was like tying up all the tangled loose ends of his life.

His relationship with the Lord changed. Despite the many times he'd wavered in his belief and even at times challenged Him, God had been right there fighting for him, not against him. Clint just hadn't been able to see it.

Hope existed.

Love existed.

And she was standing right in front of him.

"What a wonderful keepsake," Olivia said, beaming up at him. She looked as happy as if she'd found a treasure of her own.

"Keepsake? How do you figure?"

"Well, unfortunately for you, it's not one of those action figures still in its original packaging, so you can't make a million dollars selling it to the highest bidder."

"Huh." He grinned at her. "I didn't even think about that. I don't know what I'd do with a million dollars, anyway."

"The cowboy millionaire," she teased. "A rugged man who allows his wealth to grow exponentially in the bank while he and his horse and his dog continue to lead trail rides in the Deep Gulch Mountains with no one the wiser."

"I might buy a few more chickens," he said, ruffling Levi's hair. The boy smiled up at him. His two front permanent teeth were finally starting to grow in.

"And ducklings?" Caleb asked.

"Sure. And ducklings."

Olivia rolled her eyes. "Please don't put ideas into the boys' heads. I'm already in a pickle over what I'm going to do when the chickens' real owner comes looking for them. I know they don't belong to us and it's the right thing to do to give the birds back, but I hate even thinking about it. The boys will be so disappointed.

"No one is looking for the chickens," Clint assured her, holding back a grin.

"Little Horn isn't that big of a town. Unless these thieves have been stealing stuff outside our county,

Lucy will eventually find the rightful owners. Frankly, I'm surprised she hasn't already."

He laughed. "Oh, but she has."

"What?"

"Yeah. About a week ago some chickens were reported missing."

"Why didn't she come to me?"

"Because I asked her not to."

"But—"

He held up his hands. "I wanted it to be a surprise. I bought the chickens and ducklings for the boys. The birds now officially belong to Misters Levi, Caleb and Noah Kensington-Barlow."

Olivia's lips quivered and suddenly tears poured down her cheeks.

What was she bawling about?

"Are you crying?"

She sniffed and nodded, wiping her wet cheeks with the sleeve of her blouse. "I always cry when I'm happy. I can't help it."

Women. Seriously. He'd never understand them if he lived to be a hundred. But he wanted to understand *this* woman. And he wanted to live to be a hundred—with her.

"I guess I'm going to have to make it a priority to make you *cry* often."

She laughed through her tears.

"So, are we going to launch this rocket or not?" he asked the boys. "We don't have a whole lot of time before the sun sets."

"Clint. You can't!" Olivia exclaimed.

"What? Why not?"

"It's the last memento you have of the time you

and your father spent together. I thought you'd probably want to build a display case for it or something."

"It's a rocket. You don't put it in a display case. You launch it."

"I know, but—"

"It's what I want to do," he insisted. "Please. Let me do this with the triplets." He wasn't sure how much more time he was going to have with the boys. Olivia had called him in when the triplets had taken off into the mountains, but then again, search and rescue was what he did.

Did she call him because she needed him, or because of what he could do for her?

His heart clenched until he thought it might burst from his chest. He wanted to be that guy—the one she wanted when she was happy or sad, joyful, lonely or frightened. The good times and the bad.

That sounded like—

Yep. That's exactly what it was.

Love. Not just the giddy feeling when he looked at her, although there was that. But it was so much more. He was ready to commit everything to her—to commit *himself* to her.

He didn't have a ring. He had a rocket. Not exactly the most romantic idea ever.

Words had never come easy to him, and they completely failed him now. How would he ever be able to express the thoughts in his head and the emotions in his heart, tell her how much she lifted his spirit and made his soul sing?

Great. His head was spouting poetry and his mouth was apparently on strike.

Way to go, Daniels.

* * *

Olivia sat nestled on the picnic blanket her sons had brought and watched her boys launching their rocket—*all* her boys. She'd never seen Clint and the triplets so animated, except perhaps when they were building the hutch for the chickens and ducklings.

Birds she now owned, thanks to Clint. Just one more thing she owed the man. She was racking up quite an emotional bill. Every time she turned around, there he was, helping her, protecting her, supporting her.

And the way he interacted with her boys was nothing short of fantastic. There was no question that they loved him, and little doubt that he returned their affection. He was the best male role model she could possibly imagine, everything she would want her sons to emulate. He was strong and yet tender. He had confidence in himself but was always thinking of others, placing their needs first.

Placing her needs first.

She watched as Clint folded the parachute and loaded the engine in the rocket. The boys were rapt. Clint didn't care when their little fingers made mistakes. He patiently corrected them and continued building the rocket's frame.

Soon they had all the wires attached and were ready for launching. Clint cleared the area and insisted the boys move back to where Olivia sat, which was a good thirty feet from the launch pad. Keeping them safe, as always.

Holding the controller in his hand, he counted down from ten, encouraging the boys to count with him.

Ten, nine, eight...

Olivia held her breath.

Seven, six, five...

Her stomach fluttered with anticipation.

Four, three, two, one...

She was no longer watching the rocket. She was watching Clint, his golden hair shining in the sun, the shadow of whiskers on his face, his hazel eyes gleaming with exhilaration. He was reveling in this moment where the past and present came together.

Maybe even the future.

Was it possible?

Blastoff.

Her heart leaped and danced and soared as high as the rocket. There was no doubt now. She was in love with Clint. It didn't matter how or when it had happened. It only mattered that it was.

The boys shouted and danced and whooped in delight as the parachute hatched and the rocket slowly floated back to earth. That done, they lost interest and took off running down the meadow, Pav at their heels. There was so much more for a dog and three boys to explore.

They'd found the hidden treasure. And it had been Way. Way. Cool.

Olivia chuckled at their antics. Clint tossed the launch controller into the grass and jogged over to where she was sitting, then dropped down beside her with one arm behind her back.

He bent his head toward her. There was that crooked grin again. The one that made her stomach flip.

"You have no idea what this has meant to the triplets," she said, not realizing until she spoke that her voice had taken on a husky quality.

"Oh, I think I do. It's important for boys and their dads to do special projects together."

Boys and their *what*?

Her eyes widened and his gaze became more intense. He leaned in a little closer. His minty breath fanned her cheek.

"If I were a rocket designer, this one would have been different."

Olivia was still trying to wrap her mind around what Clint had just said. Or maybe he'd misspoken, or not meant it the way it had come out.

"Oh, how is that?"

He'd already moved on, talking about his rocket. She must have heard wrong.

"If I had been the one to build it, it would have reached high into the sky and then exploded into fireworks, every color of the rainbow."

"The boys would have loved that."

"Uh-huh." He leaned even closer, his lips nearly brushing her ear. "What about you?"

"Do I like fireworks? Of course."

"They're there, you know. The fireworks. Going off inside my chest." He laid his free hand over his heart. "Right here."

There might have been some ambiguity to his words but his gaze was crystal clear.

"I know I've messed up, Olivia, but every second away from you and the boys is agony for me. I've lived my entire life alone. You've shown me what it's like to have the love of a family."

She was so choked up she didn't think she could speak, but she desperately needed him to hear the words. "And the love of a woman. You have that, too, you know."

"Are you sure? I want to spend every day for the rest of my life making you happy. And I've never been anyone's role model before, but I promise I'll do everything in my power to be there for the boys. Always."

"You love them. That's really all they need."

His gaze filled with a mixture of grief and joy. "I guess I know that better than anyone." He paused and tilted his head toward her. "I do love the kids—and their beautiful mama. Will you marry me, Olivia?"

"Yes." She brushed a hand along his jaw. "Yes," she said again, breathing in the wonder of that single word. Then she laughed softly. "You took the round-about way of asking me, what with the rocket and all."

"Look who's talking, Miss Goes-Out-and-Gets-Herself-Lost so I have to find her to propose."

"I just wanted to make sure there was some chivalry in that cowboy heart of yours."

Pav returned to Clint's side and ran around the two of them, barking and wagging his tail as if he'd heard the whole conversation.

"I think Pav approves," Olivia said.

"Of my choice of a wife? Definitely. Probably not of my proposal. I'm sorry it was a rocket and not a ring. There weren't even fireworks."

"Or a million-dollar action figure."

"Yeah. Or that."

She reached for him, threading her fingers into the hair at the back of his neck and drawing him forward until his lips reached hers. "I guess we'll have to make those fireworks on our own."

* * * * *

If you liked this **LONE STAR COWBOY LEAGUE**
novel, watch for the next book,
A BABY FOR THE RANCHER, by Margaret Daley,
available March 2016.

And don't miss a single story in the
LONE STAR COWBOY LEAGUE *miniseries:*

Dear Reader,

Welcome to Little Horn, Texas! I'm so excited to have the opportunity to work on a Love Inspired six-book continuity series. I have so enjoyed working with the other authors to bring to life the community and the Lone Star Cowboy League. What a delightful blessing for readers to be introduced to wonderful authors they may not have read before.

While the Lone Star Cowboy League and the residents of Little Horn have been trying to figure out who the Robin Hood thieves are and whose baby was left at the Stillwater ranch, my heroine, Olivia Barlow, has just been struggling to keep her family together. Having feelings for rugged loner Clint Daniels only complicates matters. Love doesn't come easy, but for Clint and Olivia, it's worth the price.

I hope you enjoyed *A Daddy for Her Triplets* and the other books in this continuity series. I love to connect with you, my readers, in a personal way. You can look me up on my website at http://www.debkastner books.com. Come join me on Facebook at *http://www. facebook.com/debkastnerbooks*, or you can catch me on Twitter @debkastner.

Please know that you are daily in my prayers.

Love Courageously,

Deb Kastner

COMING NEXT MONTH FROM
Love Inspired®

Available February 16, 2016

A BABY FOR THE RANCHER
Lone Star Cowboy League • by Margaret Daley

Having discovered he's a father to a baby he never knew existed, bachelor Ben Stillwater seeks out a mother for his son. When Ben falls for pretty Lucy Benson, can he convince the busy sheriff to make room for a family?

THE RANCHER'S FIRST LOVE
Martin's Crossing • by Brenda Minton

Back in Martin's Crossing after ten years, Remington Jenkins realizes he's never forgotten the summer romance he once shared with Samantha Martin. Can he face her overprotective family once again and fight for a second chance at forever?

WRANGLING THE COWBOY'S HEART
Big Sky Cowboys • by Carolyne Aarsen

Jodie McCauley has agreed to stay at her late father's ranch until her wild horses are trained. Finding the perfect trainer leads her to Finn Hicks—the only man who's ever held her heart.

ACCIDENTAL DAD
Family Ties • by Lois Richer

Becoming the guardian of the twins his late brother hoped to adopt, rancher Sam Denver looks to the children's maternal aunt Kelly Krause for help. But when custody questions arise, they'll have to work together to keep their newly formed family intact.

THE LAWMAN'S SURPRISE FAMILY • by Patricia Johns

Police officer Ben Blake is shocked when high school sweetheart Sofia McCray returns home with a little boy she says is his son. After her newspaper job throws them together, Ben will prove he's the caring dad and husband Sofia seeks.

ALASKAN REUNION
Alaskan Grooms • by Belle Calhoune

Paige Reynolds is back in Love, Alaska, to rectify her late father's misdeeds—and introduce Cameron Prescott to the daughter she's kept hidden from him. Can Cameron forgive Paige and embrace a happily-ever-after with his first love?

REQUEST YOUR FREE BOOKS!

2 FREE INSPIRATIONAL NOVELS
PLUS 2
FREE
MYSTERY GIFTS

Love Inspired®

YES! Please send me 2 FREE Love Inspired® novels and my 2 FREE mystery gifts (gifts are worth about $10). After receiving them, if I don't wish to receive any more books, I can return the shipping statement marked "cancel." If I don't cancel, I will receive 6 brand-new novels every month and be billed just $4.99 per book in the U.S. or $5.49 per book in Canada. That's a saving of at least 17% off the cover price. It's quite a bargain! Shipping and handling is just 50¢ per book in the U.S. and 75¢ per book in Canada.* I understand that accepting the 2 free books and gifts places me under no obligation to buy anything. I can always return a shipment and cancel at any time. Even if I never buy another book, the two free books and gifts are mine to keep forever.

105/305 IDN GH5P

Name	(PLEASE PRINT)	
Address		Apt. #
City	State/Prov.	Zip/Postal Code

Signature (if under 18, a parent or guardian must sign)

Mail to the **Reader Service:**
IN U.S.A.: P.O. Box 1867, Buffalo, NY 14240-1867
IN CANADA: P.O. Box 609, Fort Erie, Ontario L2A 5X3

**Are you a subscriber to Love Inspired® books
and want to receive the larger-print edition?
Call 1-800-873-8635 or visit www.ReaderService.com.**

* Terms and prices subject to change without notice. Prices do not include applicable taxes. Sales tax applicable in N.Y. Canadian residents will be charged applicable taxes. Offer not valid in Quebec. This offer is limited to one order per household. Not valid for current subscribers to Love Inspired books. All orders subject to credit approval. Credit or debit balances in a customer's account(s) may be offset by any other outstanding balance owed by or to the customer. Please allow 4 to 6 weeks for delivery. Offer available while quantities last.

Your Privacy—The Reader Service is committed to protecting your privacy. Our Privacy Policy is available online at www.ReaderService.com or upon request from the Reader Service.

We make a portion of our mailing list available to reputable third parties that offer products we believe may interest you. If you prefer that we not exchange your name with third parties, or if you wish to clarify or modify your communication preferences, please visit us at www.ReaderService.com/consumerschoice or write to us at Reader Service Preference Service, P.O. Box 9062, Buffalo, NY 14240-9062. Include your complete name and address.

LI15

SPECIAL EXCERPT FROM

Love Inspired®

*When a woman's old love returns to town,
will she be able to resist his charms?*

Read on for a sneak preview of
THE RANCHER'S FIRST LOVE
The next book in the series
MARTIN'S CROSSING

"What are you doing here?" she asked as she stretched. When she straightened, he was leaning against the side of his truck, watching her.

"I would have gone running with you if you'd called," he said.

She lifted one shoulder. "I like to run alone."

That was what had changed about her in the years since she'd been sent away. She'd gotten used to being alone.

"Of course." He sat on the tailgate of his truck. "I was driving through town and I saw you running. I didn't like the idea of leaving you here alone."

"I'm a big girl. No one needs to protect me or rescue me."

The words slipped out and she wished she'd kept quiet. Not that he would understand what she meant. He wouldn't guess that she'd waited for him to rescue her from her aunt Mavis, believing he'd show up and take her away.

But he hadn't rescued her. There hadn't been a letter or a phone call. Not once in all of those years had she ever heard from him.

LIEXP0216

"Sam?" The quiet, husky voice broke into her thoughts.

She faced the man who had broken her fifteen-year-old heart.

"Remington, I don't want to do this. I don't want to talk about what happened. I don't want to figure out the past. I'm building a future for myself. I have a job I love. I have a home, my family and a life I'm reclaiming. Don't make this about what happened before, because I don't want to go back."

He held up his hands in surrender. "I know. I promise, I'm here to talk about the future. Sit down, please."

"I don't want to sit."

"Stubborn as always." He grinned as he said it.

"Not stubborn. I just don't want to sit down."

"I'm sorry they sent you away," he said quietly. In the distance a train whistle echoed in the night. His words were soft, shifting things inside her that she didn't want shifted. Like the walls she'd built up around her.

"Me, too." She rubbed her hands down her arms. "I wasn't prepared to see you today."

She opened her mouth to tell him more but she couldn't. Not yet. Not tonight.

Don't miss
THE RANCHER'S FIRST LOVE by Brenda Minton
available March 2016 wherever
Love Inspired® books and ebooks are sold.

www.LoveInspired.com

SPECIAL EXCERPT FROM

Love Inspired HISTORICAL

Susanne Collins has her hands full raising her brother's four orphaned children and running the farm. When cowboy Tanner Harding offers his help in exchange for use of her corrals, will he prove to be the strong, solid man she's been hoping for?

Read on for a sneak peek of
THE COWBOY'S READY-MADE FAMILY
by **Linda Ford**,
available March 2016 from Love Inspired Historical.

Tanner rode past the farm, then stopped to look again at the corrals behind him. They were sturdy enough to hold wild horses…and he desperately needed such a corral.

He shifted his gaze past the corrals to the overgrown garden and beyond to the field, where a crop had been harvested last fall and stood waiting to be reseeded. He thought of the disorderly tack room. His gaze rested on the idle plow.

This family needed help. He needed corrals. Was it really that simple?

Only one way to find out. He rode back to the farm and dismounted to face a startled Miss Susanne. "Ma'am, I know you don't want to accept help…"

Her lips pursed.

"But you have something I need so maybe we can help each other."

Her eyes narrowed. She crossed her arms across her chest. "I don't see how."

He half smiled at the challenging tone of her voice. "Let me explain. I have wild horses to train and no place to train them. But you have a set of corrals that are ideal."

"I fail to see how that would help me."

"Let me suggest a deal. If you let me bring my horses here to work with them, in return I will plow your field and plant your crop."

"I have no desire to have a bunch of wild horses here. Someone is likely to get hurt."

"You got another way of getting that crop in?" He gave her a second to contemplate that, then added softly, "How will you feed the livestock and provide for the children if you don't?"

She turned away so he couldn't see her face, but he didn't need to in order to understand that she fought a war between her stubborn pride and her necessity.

Her shoulders sagged and she bowed her head. Slowly she came about to face him. "I agree to your plan." Her eyes flashed a warning. "With a few conditions."

Pick up
THE COWBOY'S READY-MADE FAMILY
by Linda Ford,
available March 2016 wherever
Love Inspired® Historical books and ebooks are sold.

www.LoveInspired.com

Turn your love of reading into rewards you'll love with
Harlequin My Rewards

**Join for FREE today at
www.HarlequinMyRewards.com**

Earn **FREE BOOKS** of your choice.

Experience **EXCLUSIVE OFFERS** and contests.

Enjoy **BOOK RECOMMENDATIONS**
selected just for you.

PLUS! Sign up now
and get **500** points
right away!

Earn
FREE
REWARDS
Join
Today!
HarlequinMyRewards.com

MYR16R